LEGENDS FROM ALL OVER THE WORLD

Horrible Mythology: Charon

Amid the darkness and fog, a dilapidated boat is waving, slowly falling on the cold waters of the Kolya River, in front of the boat a slender old man stands as if it were a skeleton, with a pale face and cold withered eyes, about to move an oar with a pendulum.

On the opposite bank, men and women of different ages and stripes stand naked, holding their breath, their necks completely looking at the gloomy old man who came to carry them to the Kingdom of Hades, where there is a place of eternal rest. But getting on the old man's boat was not without a price, so that you could pick up a coin in the hands of the mean boats that would not allow anyone to ride for free, so for hundreds of years the ancient Greeks continued to put coin in the mouths of their dead before they were buried, and that in order for them to pay the old man's salary and move safely into the world of the dead, while those poor people who were buried without a coin in their mouths had to roam the beaches for a hundred years before the old man allowed them to board his boat, and over the course of these hundred years, many of these wandering spirits have turned into harmful vengeful demons that offend and frighten the living, sometimes out of revenge on those who have failed or put a coin in their mouths when they die.

The legend of the so-called death boats (Charon) did not leave the imagination of the ancient Greeks, they believed that he was the son of the goddess of the night Nyx, and that his only job was to transport dead wounds across the river stakes that separated the worlds of the living and the dead.

Of course, Charon would not transport his boat except for the dead, but sometimes very rarely he moved certain areas, as happened in the legend of the hero Hercules.

HORROR METHODOLOGY: POPAK

It is a mysterious predator and the other is a demon or ghoul that loves to kidnap and kill children .. In fact, even when you search in Arab or foreign studies and mythological studies, you will not find a satisfactory answer to the meaning or what it is. a scary ghost, but everyone agrees that he is an evil person who specializes in kidnapping young children.

In fact, during my research on this matter, I found that the ghost does not care about our Arab world, but rather is a common folklore among the peoples of Eastern Europe and the Mediterranean, and it is mentioned for the same purpose and purpose, i.e. the intimidation of young people in Italy and Romania as the evil creature that I will talk about today, that is, Yupaka, is also a simple distortion of the word "ghost man", especially since it gives the same meaning.

Popak is an evil skeletal creature in the shape of a stuffed or straw man, wearing a long black cloak and carrying a black bag in which he puts the children he kidnaps.

In Czech folklore, people think that bupac has an uncanny ability to pick up the voices of young children, as it sometimes imitates the sound of a child crying to lure its victims, or imitates the voice of a child friend who wants to kidnap him in order to take him out and approach. Although he is in skeletal form, he possesses immense strength and no one can escape his capture. Once he catches his prey, he puts it in a large bag, then puts the bag in a cart pulled by black cats and runs out with his precious catch.

The legend is notable for the fate of the children abducted by Popak, but most opinions agree that he blames them while they are alive.

It is widely believed that Popak only kidnaps those who misbehave, which is why Czech mothers have always scared their children with Popak.

Perhaps in the next episodes, we will look more at the frightening entities and creatures that mothers bully their young.

MYTHS ... (WOMEN) / LILITH

Origin of the label:

(Lilith) first appeared around 3000 BC. as a demon or spirit associated with winds and storms, which is why it was known as (Lilito) in (Summers) in Akkadian, while the word (Lilith) seemed to exist around 700 BC. in Hebrew knowledge in Hebrew. Where he appeared in the edition of the Bible (Old Testament) of the King (Jacob) as a demon of the night and took the form of an owl. The text refers to it as a spirit carrying a disease or wind. Both words originally (Leel) and mean night and translated literally in the sense (feminine nocturnal essence) of the term (Lilith) linguistic root in the upper and Indo-European family. The Sumerian name (Lil) is found by a representative in the name of God, wind, and storms (Anil) as well as his wife, Lady of Air (Ninel) is the hot southern wind goddess who gives women warmth during childbirth, which leads to their murder with their children (here postpartum fever is meant) and it is known that there are three evil gods in the Sumerian civilization: (Lilo) - (Lilito) - (Ardat)

Emergence of a legend :

(Lilith): demonization of Mesopotamia. Accompany the wind. It brings sickness and death with it .. The name (Lilith) appeared in the Sumerian clay disc from the city of Ur, starting in 2000 BC. Legend has it that the heavenly god ordered to plant a willow tree on the banks of the Tigris River in the city (orc). After the tree grew, the dragon took root as his home, while the terrible bird took his branches to live for him, while (Lilith) lived in the trunk of the tree. And when (Jalgamesh) the king (Orc) heard about this tree, he carried his sword and shield, killed the dragon and plucked the tree from its roots, while (Lilith) fled with the bird into the wild … Therefore, the willow tree for Lilith looks like a coffin for vampires in popular beliefs and in the ancient Sumerian beliefs (Lilith) B (Hand of Enanda) that sent mother deities (Lilith) on the roads to seduce people and bring them to the temple where sacred fertilization parties are held

(Lilith) in the Bible :.

In chapters 1 and 2 of Genesis, the following is mentioned in the story of the beginning of creation (The first created woman without a name (For contempt and intent (Lilith) Grants it (Jehovah) * With wings that allow her to escape from the Garden of Eden to separate (Adam)) However , she did not expect three angels to follow her (Sinai) And also (Cincinnati) And also (Samingilov) They find her in the Red Sea and ask her to return, but she refuses to do this, is associated with Satan, and gives birth to 100 children each day, so the angels promise to kill her children and she will hate me (Eve) And her offspring and kill the sons of Eve from humans because she raided her because (Eve) Was made of clay to replace her (Adam)

Described by :.

The description is given in the Bible (Lilith) In three texts: 1- She was described as very beautiful and very seductive and was incarnated at night in front of men to seduce them and then kill them. 2- She was described as having wings and claws, and she came at night to kill children and was summoned (b (Fatal children) 3- Described (Lilith) Also like the serpent that seduced (Adam) And also (Eve) Is with forbidden tree

Shelter :.

    1- It was mentioned in the Old Testament - Book of the Apostles - Isaiah - Chapter 34: (At the end (Edom) It is obtained by the wrath of (Jehovah) To a fiery mass of bitumen and sulfur, and before it becomes a wasteland, no one can convey it except swans, hedgehogs, owls and crows, all this takes refuge from this vacuum to find peace with wild cats, hyenas, curtains *, poisonous snakes and eagles to take (Lilito) Also her refuge) 2- Mentioned in the book (Flowers) * - Isaiah 34:14: (When he was a blessed holy man who brought destruction (Rome) Evil and turning it into ruins in order to achieve eternal life, it will send (Lilith) There it makes him settle in this ruin because it is the ruins of the world. and this is what the number indicates, and there it will settle (Lilith) She finds a place to rest) Therefore, it becomes clear to us (Lilith) Ruins and wastelands live, so that the legends of the oldest took shape (Owl) ...

Beliefs associated with the legend (Lilith).

The legend of Lilith remained prevalent among the people until the end of the eighteenth century, before this legend receded and hid in the darkness of ancient books with the beginning of (Europe) emerging from the dark ages. Many beliefs were associated with this myth, for example

Mothers made amulets for their children, especially newborns, including the names of the three angels mentioned in the legend, because they believed that (Lilith) was afraid of these names, and then fled without harming the children

Midwives did the same (soil) for mothers who are about to give birth to protect them and their children from harm (Lilita)

If an abortion occurs, everyone is sure that the mother is not pure, but possessed by the evil spirit of Lilith, so people avoid her and deny her places of worship ..

Although the fallen fetus was believed to be a winged child, because he was (Lilith's) son, so he was spared by burying him in ruins, it happened that (Simone) the woman interrupted and brought the case to court, so the judges found him really was a child but had wings

People used to draw a circle around the bed of the mother and her baby - especially if it was a man - and in the middle of the circle they draw a five-pointed star and write the names of the three angels mentioned in addition to (Adam) and (Eve) with many spells in the four corners of the camera

It was believed that if the child laughed while sleeping, this is sufficient evidence that (Lilith) is present, so one of them rushes to beat the child on the lips with one finger to leave (Lilith)

6- (Lilith) was depicted as an owl, as I mentioned earlier, and therefore the owl has always been a harbinger and destruction of the beliefs of the oldest

(Lilith) in literature: ....

Photos of literature (Lilith) in its correct form, in short: * A rebel woman who wastes herself defending her right to freedom, pleasure and equality with men * A lustful, destructive woman who strives for excellence and ability

She dealt with many literary works (the legend of Lilith), for example:

German play called (Gita) in 1565

(Paradise Lost) Milton's novel in 1667

He referred to (Lilith) using the name (adorable beard)

Victor Ojo's novel "The End of Satan" in 1886

He mixed Lilith and Isis as the daughter of Satan or a great dark woman, where he says: this is Lilith, whom we call (Isis) on the banks of the Nile. I (Lilith) (Isis) the black spirit of the world

The play (Pete of Life) (Dante Gabriel Rossetti) was shown between 1870 and 1881, and (Dante) painted (Lilith) an immortal picture whose fame applied the horizons of its time

Lilith Remy Dogormo's play in 1892

Lilith's novel by George MacDonald in 1895

The novel "God Creates First (Lilith)" (Mark Shadorn) in 1937

Lolita's novel in Lolita Galimard in 1959

Papal Gene Lawrence Doral's novel in 1983

A play (Triangle in the Ammunition Factory) (Audel Eret) in 1983, and this play also evolved into a novel with a new vision (Pierre John Jove) in 1985

Papal novel by Claude Pasteur in 1983

It is worth noting that the Austrian psychiatrist doctor …………………………………… …………………………… (Fritz Whitels) In 1932 he created a knot, which he named (Lilith knot). But oddly enough, this has nothing to do with Lilith. While the meaning of the legend, as usual, is to displace people from the path of forbidden lust by warning them to show the danger of death against them, but d ! ! .. (Fritz) surprises us with another vision, as he said that the meaning of the legend is to warn women who do not follow (Adam's) law about the fate of abandonment, sadness and eternal loss.

10 SCARIEST JAPANESE LEGENDS

1 - Lady with a cracked mouth (Kuchisake-onna)

The legend tells of a woman whose husband killed and maimed her and she split her mouth from ear to ear! ... But she came back in the form of an evil spirit covering her mouth with a medical blow, and the children may think that she is sick, but she really wants to hide this distorted mouth from sight .. When you meet one child on the street, she asks, "Am I beautiful? "! "..

If he speaks, don't kill him and cut with the scissors you are wearing !! ... And if he says "yes", you take off the mask and ask him again: "What about now?"! ". If he says, don't cut him in half, but if he says yes, his mouth will be cut just like him.

They say that the only way to avoid this evil lady's malice is to say a vague answer, that is, not yes and no, how to say: you are average in beauty, or you are not beautiful and ugly. Then the lady will be confused and don't know what to do. It is also said that if you throw a piece of candy at him, you will pick it up, and that may give you time to escape.

And some people think that she will leave the child and go her own way if he answers her the same question, saying, "Am I beautiful?" Then she will be embarrassed and left ..

This legend spread in the province of Nagasaki, It soon spread throughout Japan, It caused a lot of panic and terror at the height of its spread in the seventies of the last century, Especially after the spread of stories about the real cases of the children of this terrible lady, Some schools at that time no longer allow children returning to their homes after work, unless accompanied by an elderly person .. Who knows, there may be some truth in the story .. Therefore, I advise you, dear reader .. Always warn your children about communication with strangers.

2 - Tiki Teke:

The darkness of the night was harsh, and the streets were empty and quiet .. And this boy walked home alone and felt very agitated, because the place here is scary .. He began to accelerate his steps .. Then he noticed a girl who was looking at him from one of the windows, putting his hands on her cheek, and when he looked at her, I asked him: are you lost ?? .. Before he could answer her, the girl jumped out of the window, freezing the boy in the place of terror ..

The bottom half does not exist! .. And before he could scream, I cut him in half.

This wicked girl is truly an evil soul, and she is the most harmful to a person as she pursues him for one desire .. This is to do it like her.

They say that our heroine, Tiki Tiki, was a beautiful girl who fell on the railroad in the past, so the train came in and cut her in half .. The girl's spirit returned to take revenge, perhaps because no one helped her when she fell on handrails. The reason it is called Tiki Tiki is because she makes a sound when she pulls herself to the floor and she carries a saw with which the victim is split in two.

There is a similar Japanese legend about a girl named (Kashima Raiko), and her name is an abbreviation for a dead demon with a mask. It is said that some men raped her and subjected her to brutal torture, and when she tried to find someone who could help her, she fell exhausted over the railroad, so the train came and split it in two .. And her soul appears in public toilets and asks: where are my feet ?? ... If you answer the wrong answer, you end up cutting yourself in half, so you have to tell her that her legs are at Michen train station, and if I ask you who told you? He replied: Kashima Raiko is the one who told me .. It might leave you and your business at that time ..

I advise you to remember this story well, dear reader, if you want to go to the toilet in a public place in Japan.

3-Red Ghost (AKA MANTO):

If you are in Japan and you are anxiously looking for a toilet to meet your needs and you find empty in a public place, no luck because the toilet is one of the most suspicious places and there are many myths about it.

The legend tells of the mysterious spirit of a person who inhabits toilets, especially women's toilets, and this spirit asks the person sitting in the toilet without seeing him say, "Do you want red or blue toilet paper?"

If you answer red, the soul will cut you to pieces until your clothes turn red with your blood! ..

But if you answer in blue .. The soul will suffocate you until your face turns blue ..

The only way to avoid death is to reject any paper and answer: (I don't want paper).

4 - Red room (Akai heya)

The ads that suddenly pop up to us when we browse the Internet often don't care and close them .. But what if it was a curse that could ruin our lives! ..

The legend of the red room is not old, it is connected to the internet. This speaks of an advertising window that suddenly appears while browsing the Internet. This window contains an image with a red room or a red background, accompanied by a strange voice asking you: do you like ..? ...

If you close this window, it will reappear and this time the sound will come back to complete your previous phrase: Do you like the red room? ..

If you click again to close it, you will be presented with a list of names and your name will be among them, and it will be the last thing you will see in your life!.

They say that everyone who appeared to them in this window was found dead, and the walls of their rooms were stained with blood.

This legend first appeared in (anime) or Japanese animation as a window appeared for a boy, accompanied by the voice of a little girl who repeatedly returned the same question: Do you like red? ... Although the boy tried to stop the sound, he didn't stop, then he felt something behind him and they found him dead the next day after the walls of his room were stained with his red blood.

Of course, a dear reader might think this is just a legend, But on June 1, 2004, in Sashibo City, Nyasaki Province, an incident known as the Sharp Sasebo incident shook all of Japan for being strange, Twelve-year student, Satomi Mitarai , was killed by her 11 year old colleague Nevada !! .. The accident happened in high school during lunchtime when Nevada killed her colleague and cut her hand with a knife without pity for death! .. Why? .. Due to a small comment that Mitarai wrote on the net, she mocked Nevada, which made her angry and forced her to kill her, and when they arrested her, she said only one phrase: "Sorry."

The interesting thing about this case is that investigators found the site of the "red room" on a computer in Nevada, and some believe that this site had a demonic influence on the girl. Children usually imitate what they see.

5- Okiku Doll

It is reported that a seventeen year old boy bought a doll for his younger sister Okiko. Soon, the girl became attached to this doll and began to spend most of her play with her, But after a while the girl died for some reason, Her family decided to leave their doll as a memorial, Over time, they noticed something strange, The doll was short hair type, However, her hair got longer .. And longer .. And longer .. It even turned into the shape of long strands, and the more they cut their hair, the more it grows again.

The girl's family consulted with the priest about the strange doll, so he told them that the soul of their dead daughter had been dissolved in the doll due to her affection for her in her life.

In 1938, the girl's people gave this haunted doll as a gift to one of the temples, and it is shown there to this day, and her hair has grown to her knees, and the priests from time to time cut and clean her hair as it grows back.

6 - Kokkuri-san

Kokori - san is a game similar to Ouiju. Players write the Japanese letters Hirajana on paper, then place their fingers in the middle over a coin and ask someone a question, and then summon a spirit (Kokori) to answer them by sliding their fingers over the letters.

And just as many people believe in the Ouija game , many Japanese people believe in this game. As an important rule of the game, you should say goodbye to your soul when you're done playing by saying "Goodbye, Kokori-san" - the word of respect after the name -.

You also have to get rid of what you used to play, you have to spend this coin and write letters with a pen .. And if not, then soon failure will follow you .. And maybe death.

7 - Nopper-bo:

When we try to draw in our minds an image of a monster or a terrifying object, we often think of pointed fangs, red eyes and an ugly nose .. But have you ever imagined a face without eyes, eyebrows and nose? .. And without a mouth too !! .. Just a vague face, no features, no feelings .. Actually, it scares me as soon as I imagine it.

Nubira Po is a mythical creature in Japanese culture, also called a faceless ghost.

These ghosts are of human origin, But he can switch to Nubira Po to scare and intimidate people, They are usually harmless, They seem to the victim of a familiar person, Then their features gradually fade and their face becomes just a soft layer of skin, free of any expressions or hell. And, of course, there are many stories about this myth that I can touch on in a future article.

8 - Curse of Inukashira Park:

Inukashira Park in Tokyo is a wonderful place .. Where trees, flowers and birds sing .. It really is a great place for loved ones. If you took your bride or girlfriend there, you would definitely love it .. But .. Stay out of the garden pool! .. In order not to evaporate the love between you! ..

According to popular beliefs prevailing in Japan, renting a small boat and rowing in the waters of this pond will lead to the end of love and love between loved ones and lovers.

The origin of the legend is associated with "benzaitin", which is the Japanese name for the Hindu goddess Saraswati, whose worship moved to Japan between the 6th and 8th centuries AD through the Chinese translations she speaks of .. Benzatin is the goddess of everything that flows .. Like water. And the words .. And the rhetoric .. And the music .. And the knowledge .. They say that she watched the lakes and ponds and was jealous of the lovers who rode boats in them, and for this she cursed every couple who made a trip to her blessing in the Inukashira garden, after rowing in them, they were unhappy and the relationship between them ended.

9 - Human columns:

Human sacrifice has been practiced ever since man found his way on this earth, and his concepts and methods have varied between different peoples. In ancient Egypt, for example, beautiful women were sacrificed in the Nile River to prevent flooding.While in Japan, human bodies were used to build castles, bridges, and dams.In Japan, there are many buildings where human bones were found that belonged to people who were killed and their bodies were built. These sacrifices are based on ancient beliefs that believe that sacrificing people and using their bodies for construction will achieve a strong structure, constancy, and continuity for these buildings built on human remains.

Perhaps the most famous building believed to have been built from human bodies is Matsue Castle, located in the Japanese province of Shimane, which was built in the seventeenth century. Because parts of the castle collapsed during construction, Convinced that human bodies would help strengthen the columns of this castle, The builders looked for a suitable person in the crowd during the local Bonn festival, They selected a beautiful young woman who demonstrated her wonderful dancing skills, They kidnapped and killed her then they used her body to build a wall and they completed the castle without any accidents getting in the way. It seems that the spirit of this dancer returned after the completion of the construction and inhabited the castle, and for this, according to the legend, the structure of the castle vibrates whenever a girl dances in the street near the castle, and for this the government issued a law prohibiting dancing on this street! ...

10 - Dog with a Human Face (Jinmenken)

The relationship between humans and dogs has always been strong, as the dog is known to be man's best friend. But with jinmenkin dogs, things are a little different since he has a human face and can talk, and if you get close to him, you will ask you to leave him alone! .. He was known as a harbinger of pessimism and was blamed after accidents and disasters, and the locals often saw it at night.

Recently, stories of dogs with a human face have increased, with many witnesses claiming to be following them. At first glance, they thought they were normal dogs, But they soon took notice of her human faces and often saw her hiding in the middle of the garbage at night, Most messages are limited to suburban and rural areas, But sometimes you see in urban areas, especially near high-rise residential complexes, as well as in garbage cans behind restaurants in densely populated areas. There is also evidence that these human dogs chase cars very quickly on dark highways and that they are capable of speeds up to 100 kilometers per hour and make noise like strange screams.

It is believed that jinmen are the souls of poor dogs who were hit by cars, or evil spirits embodied in the form of dogs. There are those who see this as a result of biological experiments carried out in secret laboratories, as well as those who can run from monkeys rather than dogs. Monkeys are more like animals in humans.

finally ..

Japan is not like Korea or China, as some people think, since each country has its own culture and civilization .. And of course its legends .. Now that you have finished reading what I have presented to you in this article ... How many of you would like to go to Japan? ...

JINX MYTHS

"don't do it .. This is bad." .. A phrase that has been heard for a long time from an early age, and we are interested in doing certain things, usually the elderly and relatives call this a warning, waving their fingers. According to this phrase, a set of prohibitions and misfortunes from which a person must move away and avoid, so as not to return him with suffering, evil eye and suffering. People are divided over these warnings, there are those who laugh at them and mock them, and there are those who believe in them to such an extent that it disturbs his imagination and loses his life.

I personally remember that at some point in my life I was very careful to be my first step when I left the house with my right foot and open the door and close it with my right hand, even though I was left-handed and this has long turned into into an obsession with me .. He is obsessive .. It doesn't always depend on popular heritage, but people can sometimes create their own shapes and patterns from these obsessions, for example, if someone thinks that wearing a certain shirt brings him luck, otherwise that he sees him in the morning brings him the evil eye.

In general, human memory retains a large and varied number of such warnings that people fear and avoid.

Evil Eye:

According to the dictionary, envy is the desire for grace to disappear from others. In other words, the ability of the eye to harm others, and for this the envious eye is called the evil eye. The belief in jealousy is rooted in our Arab region, and is rooted in the foot. It is known that in Pharaonic Egypt Ain Horus envied, and in Sumer they hung amulets on the doors of houses for the same purpose. And the Arabs in Al Jahliyah flew from Al Ain, especially colorful ones. Envy is mentioned in the Noble Qur'an.

To prevent jealousy, people can do strange things, such as if some of them give their children ugly names, so you see one of them call his son "Zabala"! .. It is so that the eyes of envious people do not understand this, and there are those who wear their little boyish clothes and lengthen their hair, especially when the boy is handsome or neglects his cleanliness, even thinking that he sees him as a vagabond, .. All this is for in order to prevent the evil eye-. They can prevent infertile women from entering their homes so that their children are not jealous, even unintentionally .. These and other things were not alien to our societies in the past, especially with regard to children as they died a lot due to lack of medicine and a doctor, and it was the firm belief that the child's illness and death were caused by an envious eye. Even today it is not strange to hear how angrily hesitates, carrying his sick child, saying: "They envied him ... Yesterday he had nothing!".

There are other things people can do to protect themselves from envy, such as paper, hanging amulets, wearing locks, hanging old shoes in a new car, and painting the wall of a new home with the victim's blood. Perhaps the five, which are hand-shaped in the middle, is an open blue eye that is attached to houses and cars and can be worn like a necklace that gave rise to the old saying, "Five five." Incense and sand is another remedy used to bring back the envious eye, as some housewives soared their homes to protect their loved ones while chanting, "The envious eye has a stick."

Religious scientists have different opinions about the evil eye, Some see that people's understanding and awareness of the problem of envy is very wrong, The eye of people cannot harm others apart from the will of the Creator, This is God who values and does things, Therefore, under the prohibition of envy and preventing it it is understood that a person arises from bad and evil thoughts, And that his brother suffers only from good and love, It is inappropriate for a good believer to hide evil in his heart.

It is worth noting that not all envy is reprehensible, There is something like this, Mahmoud, This is a delight, It means looking at the blessings in the hands of others, not wanting to take them away, As if you are striving to become rich, like your neighbor, you make him rich but you do not envy him and do not want to lack, Or you want to become a doctor like your brother to be followed and admired. There are those who believe that if it were not for envy, which generates competition, humanity would not have reached its paper development.

black cat:

Cats tend to like pets, but at the same time, they are mysterious and sometimes frightening, especially when we see a black cat sitting silently on the side of the road, continuing to look at us .. This is what scares the hearts of those who believe that the black cat is not just a beautiful and innocent animal, but rather a disguise and disguise used by supernatural beings such as genies, demons and demons to enter and manipulate the human world.

Beliefs about the black cat are ancient and widespread in all parts of the earth. In western folklore, there was a constant connection between the black cat and magic, and they believed that black cats were the servants of witches. And they believed that the passage of a black cat blocking a person's path was a bad omen and could be a sign of his death. In the East, some people believed that the black cat was the embodiment of the genies, and that the genie appeared in the form of a black cat to approach and carry people. Others claim that the bodies of black cats are a haven for goblins to live in after dark.

And in magic, they mentioned the strange properties of black cats, and they said that eating their meat rotates the magic, he mentioned that he speaks in his animal where he says: "And the public claims that whoever ate the black senator did not did magic. " And he went to such a dummy in his book Animal, where he says: "The civilian feline who ate black meat from him did not work with magic. Al-Kazzini said: the bitterness of the lions and the bitterness of the black chicken, if they dry up and are crushed, and they suffer from them if the genie appeared to him and served him. He said: "He is being judged."

Crow:

He is the smartest of all birds, but this did not intercede for him in people, since many of them look at him with suspicion and pessimism .. Perhaps to suppress his voice and body, and hate and regret, and because he is a trash animal that lives on carrion and corpses. This aversion to crows dates back to ancient times. In England and Ireland, they considered the raven to be the embodiment of the gods of war and the vow of death. In Sweden, they believed that ravens were the souls of people who died dead, and in Denmark, they considered them to be evil spirits expelled from possessed bodies. As for the Arabs, they saw in the raven the full embodiment of pessimism and suffering, and the speaker talks to us about this in his book "The Animal", saying:

"And for the sake of their pessimism with the crow, they were taken from his name, alienation and alienation. And there is no rest on earth, no overthrow, no place, no blind eye, no anything to which they are pessimistic, except that the crow was upset about it.

And because it is the embodiment of evil and pessimism, it is not surprising that the crow is present in many horror films, where we see him accompanying evil witches and living in abandoned places and residential buildings, People can be brutally attacked, as he did in the film " Birds "by unique international director Hitchcock in 1963, Or it could bring them back to life from the grave, As in the famous 1994 film The Raven, Considered by some to be a sign of the crow's misfortune, He witnessed one of the strangest incidents in film history During the filming of the viewer, actor Michael Massey had to shoot Brandon Lee in order to kill him.The pistol that would fire was real, but his bullets were freed from gunpowder.However, the crew in charge of the weapon apparently forgot to empty one of bullets, and they set off, presenting a scene, to take up residence in Brandon's bowels and kill him. There are those who believe that the incident was planned to end the life of the young actor, as happened to his father, martial arts star Bruce Lee.

Pour hot water into the bathroom:

People believe that pigeons are the dwelling of jinn, This is the only place in the house where people do not live at home, People do not prolong their stay in it and do not accept it as advice or a bed to sleep, It is the only place where prayer is not performed, and the name God is not mentioned, The only place where people remain naked is my Lord, how you created me without shame and shame ... No wonder that after all this the genie takes home and home for him! .. Therefore, when working with the bathroom, care must be taken so that its invisible inhabitants do not accidentally get hurt, Pouring hot water into the bathroom at night can affect the genies that live in it, Or one of his children may be killed, Especially if the purr has forgotten to be called the Merciful and seek refuge with Satan, which makes the genie take revenge on the person in every possible way and can wear him.

Of course, there are those who laugh at the fullness of this myth, and there are also those who firmly believe in its truth, and people have many stories that they contemplate touching upon pouring hot water into the bathroom.

Open scissors:

Leaving it open brings bile, a myth that some believe. Not only that, but opening it and closing it unnecessarily, that is, having nothing to cut it down is also bad and can lead to innumerable calamities and troubles. Contrary to this myth, there are those who believe that scissors can provide protection, especially if they are placed under a pillow while sleeping, as this prevents nightmares.

It is not known how these scissors myths originated, possibly because scissors are a harmful tool that can lead to serious accidents if left open or played with children. For your information, these myths are not only related to the East, In the West, they have their own notes, They believe that breaking the scissors of the blade is very bad and a harbinger of disaster, And the fact that using scissors on the first day of New Year brings misfortune throughout years, And these hanging scissors open over the threshold will prevent magicians and demons. They also believe that scissors should never be presented as a gift because it will ruin the relationship with the person they are for.

Inverted outsole:

Many people usually do not leave their shoes or soles upside down, that is, the heel up. Personally, the phrase "turn your slippers, please" was often passed on to me by ear in my house, and how many shoes and soles I turned over as a child! .. But I honestly didn't understand at the time why I should turn the shoe or the sole back into the correct position .. Does it have something to do with pessimism? ..

Some deny that this myth is associated with pessimism and flying, but they claim that they leave the shoes upside down, that is, its dirty and dirty end to heaven, in which there is no insult to the divine self, and it is said that angels do not enter home if there is an inverted sole. Of course, this is a myth that has no origin and no religious support, but it is popular with people and some may harden it. There are also those who argue that the origin of the myth is related to fitness and etiquette, because the heel of shoes or slippers is usually dirty, so an inverted look is undesirable.

Eye Penetration and Tinnitus:

The shelf of the eye and its penetration can be a bad oath or a good oath, according to the raised eye, and if left, he is pessimistic, but if he is right, this is good news.

It is difficult to find a logical explanation for this myth, it can be associated with the left and right, since people from ancient times have always looked with optimism on the right side and pessimism on the left, and the Arabs flew to the left. As far as science is concerned, blinking eyes has nothing to do with pessimism or happiness. These are nothing more than involuntary abductions caused by eye infections or lack of sleep and fatigue.

There is a similar myth about ringing in the ears of the ear, which is why they said that the buzzing of the right ear means there are those who praise you and praise you, while the left tinnitus means that there are those who rape you and receive from you. Aside from the myth, medical tinnitus could be evidence of ear infections or high blood pressure, or prolonged exposure to noise.

Cut your nails at night:

If you want to cut your nails at night, don't be surprised if you hear someone tell you that they hate it, and like the rest of the myths we have mentioned, it is unknown what a face of hate is when cutting nails at night. Some have tried to link the issue to religious heritage, although there is no evidence or evidence to indicate a ban on cutting nails at night. There are also those who associate matter with magic.It is known that the magician needs a part of the victim's body in order to perform magic.This part is usually a lock of hair or a nail clipper.For this reason, wire cutters are warned in the trash can, It is advisable to bury him. So that someone does not grab it and use it to create harmful magic, Especially if we know that magicians are active and know at night under the cover of darkness.

Number 13:

Perhaps this is the most famous myth in the world, because many people in the West and East do not rest from this number, they never want to wear number 13 or live in a house or apartment with this number. In some societies, this fear has turned into a kind of phobia that everyone wants to take into account, even if they do not believe in it, especially in the West, where the myth was originally created, Do not be surprised, dear reader, if you enter Amara once and climb lift and you won't find number 13 in the floor numbers. In some cities they change the numbering of the thirteenth floor to (12 A), .. Or they can completely cancel it, so you see that the number 14 comes just after 12, because no one wants to live or work on floor 13. And because of the intensity of their pessimism on this day, they avoid marriage, and they are especially pessimistic if it happens on the 13th of the month on Friday.

Of course, not all people believe in this myth, most of them laugh at it and consider it worthy of fools, but to be honest, it is still very popular, sometimes even those who do not believe in it avoid it, no one wants to judge destiny. Historians and scholars disagree on the origin of this myth. One of the most correct opinions that you attribute to the last dinner of Christ, as the number of those sitting at the table was 13, Christ and his twelve dialogues, and one of these disciples (Judas) was a traitor who betrayed Christ to the priests in exchange for their house, numbered, and for this reason people are pessimistic about this number.

There are also those who believe that the incident with the death of Abel by his brother Cain occurred 13 months later.

The ancient Scandinavian tribes have a legend about a meeting attended by twelve deities of their deities, and the thirteenth deity Loki was not invited to him, so this hostile deity, which we saw in the movie Thor 2011, returned and avenged the murder of one of deities.

The number of gallows is said to be 13.

In the old Persian calendar, the thirteenth day of the New Year was considered the day of the evil eye. To this day, Iranians still spend the thirteenth day of the New Year (Nowruz). What they call "Badr" will be celebrated in parks and public squares because they believe that staying at home on this day brings the evil eye.

Myth # 13 has no origin in Arabic culture, but it was sought after among people in the twentieth century as a result of friction in the West.

THE LEGEND OF THE LOVE THAT MADE LIFE

Several centuries ago, when souls were pure and dreams of people were simple and naive, a Greek sculptor named Jamilon lived in Cyprus. He was so proficient in his art that the statues he carved were almost alive, but despite the fame of his colleagues and the popularity of his craft, Gamalon lived alone and was never married. He had a deep and innate disgust for women who thought they were the source of all misery and that being away from them was a prey because they were deceiving and unfulfilled, so he lived alone, only forgetting the ways of his loyal colleague.

There is no doubt that a person's aversion to something that is based on negative personal experience, and legend tells us that the total hatred of women was caused by his contacts with local prostitutes in his city .. Perhaps he thought that all women are so cheap, and that all of them, without loyalty, pass from one breast to another in exchange for money, and for this he decided to make his own version of a woman, a clean copy, free of impurities and defects that he saw in other women, and thus unleashed their colleagues to create a sculpture that was not. The world sees an example of her in terms of splendor and beauty.

With aesthetics, he devastated all the arts and crafts that he had on this statue, which he made of ivory and named it Galatia, and when he finally finished making his wonderful masterpiece, he stood for a long time, and the more he pondered it. the more he admired and fascinated him, until he finally fell ill with the disease from which he had always fled and tried to avoid .. He became a lover .. Ironically, he loved the statue made by hand! ...

She clung to Gamalion with a statue of Galatia, which was increasing day by day, and he flirted with her face with his fingers and took her lips, covering her with luxurious clothes, bringing her gifts and flowers, talking to her, outliving her, and blinking his eyes with tears when he leads to the suffering of his beautiful heart .. Galatia has filled her life with the air he breathes, and it became impossible to live without it.

Bad with aesthetics ... How he wanted in his retreat for Galatia to turn into a real woman .. How much he begged the gods to have mercy on his beloved heart and breathe life into this solid, solid body ..

It seems that some of these pleas and slander heard the gods, shared his fortune, and worked to fulfill his desires.

On the day of the celebration of the feast of the Lord of Love Aphrodite (Venus), he carried a total of his sacrifice to the temple and threw it into the sacred fire, so he saw how the flames rise three times higher, as evidence of the acceptance of his sacrifice and a sign from heaven for something that Gamalon did not immediately realize.

That night, Jamilun returned to his home and kissed the statue of Galatia, as he did when he returned home, but this time I felt something different, Galatia's lips were softer and her body was softer and hotter. Aphrodite answered Gamalion's pleas and she breathed life into Galatia's body, and the statue finally became a living woman of flesh and blood.

The legend ends with a wonderful marriage with Galatia. According to the Roman poet Ovid, who passed on the legend to us, Galatia gave birth to Jamilun, a boy named Paphos, the name of his campaign later in the holy city of Aphrodite in Cyprus.

The legend of Gamalion has a wonderful meaning as it tells us that whenever we love something with our hearts, we can resurrect life and turn it into a great thing. Love works wonders, not only love between men and women, but even our love for our studies, work or hobbies ... All of this can lead to great results when it is associated with honesty and determination.

The myth of Greek aesthetics has been viewed by modern writers in a more realistic and logical way. The satirical Irish writer George Bernard Shaw wrote his famous play Begmalion in 1912, inspired by Greek myth. The heroine of the play is a poor girl who sells flowers on a street called Eliza, Professor Henry Huygens bets that he can turn her into a cool public lady without anyone noticing, and indeed he trains and teaches her for several months , in the end he succeeds in his mission with great success, but the game (It doesn't end happily like a legend, Professor Higgins (With aesthetics) This is about Eliza (Galatia) From a disadvantaged girl immersed in a woman of high society, he does not marry in the end who made his hands, but Eliza rebelled against the domination and stubbornness of the professor, leaving him to marry a poor young man like her.

The great Egyptian writer Tawfiq al-Hakim A also wrote a play called Begmalion, and he wrote more attentively and adherent to Greek myth than Bernard Shaw. The play Tawfiq Al-Hakim comes with us with a legend, which leads to the reaction of the gods to the prayers of Jamilon and the blow of life in the body of Galatia. What happens next is more complex than what the legend has given us, and more realistic. Life does not always become happy, and some must experience a relationship of love, however strong it may be, eventually apathy and some doubts, suspicions and fears .. Thus, we see that the aesthetics in the play are suspicious of the actions of his beautiful wife Galatia. and he thinks that she is cheating on him with his friend Narcissus, so he asks the gods to return her to the statue as she was, but the gods work to reveal her innocence and bridge the gap between the spouses, and despite this, Gamalon insists for the gods to return her to her first body, that is, to the statue, and the reason is that he no longer sees the perfect beauty created by his colleagues, only an ordinary woman, hold a broom and cook food.

The gods answer the request aesthetically and return Galatia to the statue, but with aesthetics, he soon misses his wife and again calls on the gods to turn Galataia into a living woman, but the gods refuse this time, and in a fit of anger, Gamalon smashes the statue and then dies of of a broken heart.

I think that the lesson or the meaning of my play, Bernard Shaw and Tawfiq Al-Hakim, is that it is impossible to achieve perfection, there is no perfect woman, since there is no ideal life that is not full of difficulties and troubles .. Long-term happiness, eternal love and utopias exist only in the minds of delusions such as the myth of Greek aesthetics.

7 WAYS TO GET RID OF BAD LUCK

Sprinkle with salt:

Salt is used as a remedy for bad luck in many cultures and religions, and is the most powerful and quickest way to destroy magic. It is said that whoever uses it should hold it a little and spread it on the left side, it will help get rid of the evil eye, but be careful, because if it is accidentally scattered on the right side, it will bring more evil eye!. There are also those who take a hot bath with salt, it is enough to put two large tablespoons in the bath to cleanse the body of all negative waves.

Incense:

Incense is considered one of the rituals prevalent in the Levant as a whole, and it was known from the time of the pharaohs in Egypt, as well as in America until Columbus, and India, where it was used, in particular, in temples and religious rituals that were prevalent at that time. and it still carries religious connotations even today, where it is considered to bring goodness and blessing, and protection from eyes and envy. Good and potent species are chosen for taste, such as sandalwood and jasmine, and burned until they give off steam and a pleasant scent, and are often used on occasions when family and friends meet, such as weddings and celebrations.

Famous Symbols for Attracting Envy:

Khamisa: Khamisa is an anti-envy mantra and is an open palm tree with five fingers, which are usually made of silver or copper and are very popular in Arab society, especially Moroccan, where women often use it during pregnancy and for a baby at birth.

Plate (horseshoe): An ancient belief from the primitive ages that has been associated with horses and related goods and benefits for humans since ancient times, and the Greeks believed that its semicircular shape symbolized fertility and good luck.

Pattern: This is a hand with an eye attached to the neck, this eye is said to accumulate the negative energy of an envious look that falls on a person by others.

Gems:

Usually stones and crystals have many useful characteristics, as a person keeps them in their home, or women carry them as jewelry to decorate when attending family events or parties, and these are some examples of their characteristics according to popular belief. :

Agate: Used against the evil eye, it also maintains focus, strengthens relationships, and reduces fear.

Turquoise: attracts money, success and love, relaxes the mind, relieves stress, and promotes friendship and increased luck.

Coral: It is said to cure certain skin conditions such as psoriasis and is also used to treat envy and neglect.

Prayer or prayer:

People of different religions see that petition and petition to God or gods fulfills their desires and hopes, especially if it was preceded by the hope of wiping away sins and sins, and its owner thanks and praises for blessings that would also change a person's opinion of his condition and also look on the entire side of the bowl, that is, he will begin to think positively about him and forget his fears.

Travel:

Some people think that travel helps to eliminate bad luck because he goes with the person to a distant place and disappears, so he does not return with him when he returns!.

It also gives the feeling that it is not responsible for its poor condition, but perhaps its location .. Like a country, house, street or workplace .. This is the reason.

Break the egg:

Earlier, I read a topic about this on the website of the Department of Realistic Experiences, where the author talks about her recovery from an illness from which she suffered from an egg. And I discovered that the source of this myth is the voodoo religion in West Africa and the southern United States. This belief believes that eggs expel evil spirits, as they are widely spread in Mexico, when the person in charge of the treatment transfers the egg several times to the patient's body to absorb negative energy from it, and then breaks it into a glass of water. The patient went over to the egg.

EVIL IN THE WATER

The vast seas and oceans have psychological implications that vary from person to person.Some may find it comfortable to listen to the sounds of quiet waves on the beach, while others relate to their cold chills as they imagine that the creatures under that water might be, oh which we know nothing, This mystery in the seas has delighted people with its imagination of what lies in its depths, and if you want to know some secrets, listen carefully to those who travel the seas and oceans far away. They are the ones who mix their reality with their imaginations due to what they have gone through and seen in these oceans, and often they end up. Their lives drowned in the darkness of these depths … I will tell you some myths from different countries about the monsters that live in this darkness while they wait for people to approach these mysterious waters …

Frog (Water)

"This tobacco is for you, sir. Fodnik, please give me the fish."

This was what some fishermen say to get fish and then put tobacco in the water.

But who is this vodka they are praying for ??

According to Slavic myths, this creature lives in rivers, ponds and streams and looks like an old man with a frog with a green beard that extends down his legs and long hair, Covered in mud, algae and the skin of black fish, The hands of frogs are enough and he has the tail is like a fish, and its eyes look like they are cutting coal. Locals call him grandfather and they say that when he gets angry, he breaks dams and watermills and drowns animals and people, so residents always blame him when someone drowns or floods, and for this also many hunters and mills try please him by making sacrifices. It is said that he disguises himself as a beautiful flower in order to attract girls to him, and when they approach him, they arrest them and then kidnap them to his kingdom underwater and force them to marry him and serve him.

On the other hand, some believe that this creature is not harmful at all, and sometimes it can appear when playing cards with people of the same gender! Or sit silently over the rocks, and there are fishermen who value and respect this creature and exchange tobacco with him as a gift to help him fish.

According to Slavic myths, this creature is a soul that used to be a living person, but drowned in suicide.To get rid of this creature, the water must be blessed in the river or pond in which it lives, because it is afraid of holy water. water, no one has seen it, so some believe that it is fatal to him and cannot live in him.

Sea horse (each yuzge):

When the name "sea horse" is mentioned, it is often crossed by a cute sea animal that looks like a horse in checkerboard stones, but this name is not limited to this little creature, but rather has other meanings that spread and spread to the world of myths and mysteries .. According to the astronomer Catherine Briggs, the legend of the sea horse that we will now talk about, has its roots in Scotland, where this horse or this spirit is considered the most dangerous type of horse.

This creature lives in the seas and lakes and is able to change its shape, since it can disguise itself as a horse, pony, a beautiful person or huge birds ... And if one of them ascended, this creature appeared in the form of a horse, he is not in danger as long as he walked on the ground, But if he comes to the water, it means the tragic end of this passenger, Because the horse's skin will become like a sticker, so that the passenger cannot escape, and this horse will jump with the victim into the deepest point of the water until he breathes with his last breath, and then tears apart the victim's body and devours him, except for the liver, which will float on the surface of the water as a sign of the terrible fate that its owner met.

This rogue creature can disguise itself as a handsome man and can only be identified by his hair, as silt, sand, and water weeds will be stuck with him. Because of this creature, the inhabitants of the highlands of Scotland are afraid to approach animals or strangers they see off the coast.

The blacksmith reportedly lost his daughter to this creature, so he decided to take revenge, and with the help of his son, he set a trap of sharp hooks and then roasted the sheep on these hooks until they turned red.Soon the smell of fried meat attracted this creature and finally emerged from the water as he wrapped himself around him in a thick fog in search of the source of the smell.As soon as I approached the sheep, mourning and his son accelerated and they put hooks into his body.After a short struggle, his body became motionless , and in the morning nothing of the creature was left except the gel.

Sea Monk (Umib ō zu):

This monster in Japanese folklore represents the worst nightmares that hunters and sailors can have in Japan, and the word meaning of his name is "Buddhist sea monk", he lives in the oceans and sinks ships of sailors who dare to pronounce his name. ,.

His head is said to be a large circle similar to the heads of shaved monks, his body is huge black and large eyes, and this is considered the type of devil who hides with fishermen, crashes their ships and drowns them. According to legend, when Ombuzu gets angry, the team will be asked to give him a barrel to fill with seawater and pour it over them. To avoid this fate, he needs to be given a bottomless barrel and his time will try to drown them again and again without being used, giving them time to save their lives.

Although the Pacific Sea is the best thing any sailor wants, But for those who believe in Umbuzu, they see this deceptive calm as a prelude to the appearance of a demonic beast, so you can see that they never feel comfortable when the sea is calm. calm can turn from a moment into a wild storm. The exit of the beast is usually accompanied by strong winds and strong waves.

This myth is associated with Japanese thought, which believes that the sea is the last refuge for people who are dying and there is no one to take care of them.

Water Mage (Finfolk):

People have always dreamed and imagined what their life would be like underwater, and the legends associated with mermaids have played a fundamental role in fueling people's imaginations .. But you should think carefully before you wish .. Some dreams are better for them to remain dreams. ...

Finn Falk is a legend that spread to the islands in northern Scotland about wizards living in a big city deep in the water called the City of Wizards (Finfolkaheem) .It is a city surrounded by colorful algae. It is said that it never gets dark, because the glow of the sea animals illuminate them at night, Halls and rooms are decorated with curtains that move with the movement of streams.

These amphibious mages possessed many special abilities, such as changing their forms, but their weak point was silver metal as they never came close to coins or silver jewelry. They moved freely between their world and the human world at the top for centuries and with one goal: to kidnap people and force them to marry them and spend the rest of their lives serving them and doing housework.It was not motivated by love or love. but greed and lust for possession of people. To arrest their prey, witches disguise themselves as a sea animal, a plant or article of clothing floating on the surface of the water, The disguised magician approaches his target, or rather his prey, carefully so that he can grab it, Sometimes the male appears as a fisherman in a boat. As for the woman, she takes the form of a nymph with golden hair, white skin, unspeakable beauty, and a wonderful singing that overcomes doors.

Currently, no one sees them, and the locals believe that it was the people who left the pagan worship that led to their disappearance.

Giant snake (Abaya):

Evil for humans can be beneficial to other creatures, and this is exactly what revolves around the Milanese myth ... Abaya is a huge magic sea snake that lives on the bottom of freshwater lakes in Fiji, the Solomon Islands and Vanuatu.

This snake considers all the creatures in the lake to be its children, as it protects and fiercely protects them from anyone who wants to harm them.Many fishermen tried to hunt in these lakes, But one blow from this creature's tail caused a high wave that destroyed their ships and boats.

In another version of the legend, they say that Abai's strength and anger are more than a blow of the tail, This suggests that once a man found a pond full of fish, and at the bottom there was a snake Ebay, But the man did not know his existence, After that As he caught a lot of fish, he returned to his village and told everyone about his discovery of this lake, so everyone went fishing, Even a woman of them hunted Abai, but he managed to escape from it. After what happened, Abai's anger increased significantly and caused the sky to fall violently, so the water level in the lake rose, and the whole village and its inhabitants drowned, except for one woman who did not eat from this fish, so she hung a tree and survived the drowning...

Although Abai's magical power may come from human imagination and fear of the unknown, many people still believe in the presence of giant snakes living in the lower lakes.

Sea Monster (Leviathan):

This monster is the most famous monster from the depths, and when we say that the most famous of them, we mean the worst and most evil of them .. This is the closest thing to Satan himself, and it has been mentioned in many historical religious books and books. myths with different names, Including the name of the Dragon Sea, He often floats above the water, He will serve as the ruler for all creatures that live in the sea, His skin looks like a layer of overlapping and sharp shields, He ignites smoke from his gills and fire from his mouth.

And, based on his description in ancient Egyptian myths, he is a legendary crocodile-like animal and was the enemy of the God Horus. And in Jewish beliefs, he wrote that "Leviazan" is a dragon woman who lives in the depths with the monster of the earth (Behemoth) and will make a banquet out of her flesh for the righteous after the end of her life. According to one of the ancient Jewish captains, during one of his trips on the ship, he saw the head of Leviathan and wrote horns on it: "I am one of the most sinister creatures in the sea, and my height reaches 300 kilometers."!

And when this terrible creature feels hungry, it comes out of the mouth with intense heat, which makes the sea water boil. And his residence is the Mediterranean. Another story says that he swallows a whale every day and emits his eyes with a light similar to the glow of the sun when it shines.

Despite Leviathan's superpower, he fears a type of worm called "Kilbett", where these worms stick to his gills and then feed on them.

Eclipse of the Dragon (Bakunawa):

Dolphins and whales can jump over water in the air .. But how far can the monsters that live in the water jump ?! Can they reach the sky, for example? ! ,, In ancient times in the Philippines, people believed that Batala created 7 moons to light up the sky, but the dragon Bakonawa who lives in the sea was very impressed by these luminous moons and attracted their beauty, so he went out of the ocean to the sky and swallowed moon until the seventh moon remained, which angered the "Batala", "A lot, People from Bakunava wanted to spit out the moons and prevent him from swallowing the last moon, so they left the house with pots and dishes and made a loud noise so that he could feel fear And some people in the villages played quiet music so that he could sleep in deep sleep, then kill him and take away the moons, Bakunawa was known as a "collar eater" as well as a "man eater" Filipinos believe he is responsible for the lunar eclipse as it is still trying to absorb the seventh moon .. That is, the moon that we all see every night.

In another story, Bakunava is said to have had a sister who looked exactly like a sea turtle and was going to an island in the Philippines to lay eggs, but the locals noticed that the sea water followed her whenever she went to the island to lay eggs, which reduced the size of the island and felt anxiety that their island would eventually disappear, so they killed it.When Bakunawa found out about what had happened to his sister, he wanted revenge, ascended into heaven and devoured the moons, The inhabitants were afraid and prayed to "batale" to punish this dragon, but he refused to punish him and told them that they must make noise, brutally beating pans and dishes to disturb him, Then Bakonava vomited the moons, disappeared and no one saw him again, They say that the island on which the turtle lay is still present in the Philippines.

Others believe that Bakunawa fell in love with a human girl, and when the leader of her tribe knew this, they burned down their home, so Bakunawa got angry, ascended to heaven and ate six moons, but Batala defeated him and banished him far from the sea so that the seventh moon would not devoured, People believe that a lunar eclipse occurs when Bakunawa tries to return to his homeland again.

SNAKE'S SON

This story took place in a remote village in the east of Algeria, in a distant place where the hand of civilization did not reach after due to the complexity of the terrain and the distance from the civilized center. There, in this village, a woman lived with her husband, a husband who was not like other men, was cruel and cruel with his wife, because he simply did not have children, and this shortcoming was the reason for his violent behavior. He always beat and brutalized her for the most trivial reasons, and the harsh living conditions exacerbated other wounds for the poor woman.

One day the husband came to roar and asked his wife to have supper for a group of his companions and take meat with him to prepare a meal, and then he left, the wife began to cook dinner, but the poor woman did not know what was waiting for her while she was busy cooking the snake. sneaked into a dilapidated kitchen and fell into a pot in which broth was boiling, and because the house was not equipped with electricity, because the village was remote and far away, the poor wife did not notice what happened due to poor lighting and her quick participation in the preparation due to for fear of her husband's oppression if she is late. In this, after a while, the husband is banned with his companions, and the woman puts in food, and the men soon seemed to be eating, but they noticed that the taste and shape of the meat varied from one piece to another, and soon the topic became clear and you you can imagine the violent revolution of the husband, after the owners left upset, he started beating his wife and didn't get enough, but bring his gun and his kindness between eating snake meat and killing him with bullets.

The poor woman did not find what she was doing, she was alone and weak and had no choice. Death is one. She decided to eat meat and expected death every day, but the amazing thing is that she did not die, and what happened was not expected. She became pregnant, and they do not believe her husband, because he did not have children. Of course, as usual, the men accused his wife of treason and any betrayal .. He accused her of being in the stomach because of the snake she ate, and that the one in her stomach was the son of a snake, and the poor woman was silent and patient.

Of course, a man like this uneducated and cruel husband probably thought so, and he waited for the date of birth to kill the monster, as he says, and the decisive hour came, and women came from the village and began their work, not knowing the truth in this question, while the alleged husband continued to wait and wait, and after a short time he heard the cry of a small creature rushing ... But suddenly he heard another voice, the female Zagared was pleased with the newcomer.

The man shouted at them, demanding silence and raising a pistol, asking them to come in to kill the child, but the women prevented him because his wife told them her story when she was on the birth bed, so the women rose up and shouted at the man's face, saying that if you want to kill a child, so first look at him, the man looked in the eyes of anticipation for a small object. He was a wonderful child with blush cheeks filled with white health, such as beautifully creative milk. Glory to his creation. The man stood confused or indecisive, but the women woke him up from confusion. They drove him out of the evil of exile because he offended his poor, patient wife, and the woman lived with her child in the village, but she could not forget that her husband offended her, and she called her child in the name of Garib, who is the son of a snake , because the real snake is her cruel, unjust husband who will not have mercy on her weakness and patience.

Dog people, headless people and a one-eyed nation .. Strange creatures between legend and history

We've heard a lot about strange creatures in our world, and at first glance I thought they were just legends, but there is a rule that every legend has its origin in history.

From what we've heard about:

A newcomer, a myth that arose from giant birds that already lived in deep time and are now extinct. Dragon, and this could be due to some types of old flying dinosaurs or giant snakes that live in the forests. There are many other famous creatures that have dominated the world of myth.

But have you heard of the beheaded men ?? ..

At first glance, you will see how their paintings are painted, the dear reader expects, and you will be sure that these are legends that were painted on the walls, like other myths that people of ancient civilizations used to paint on their walls.

But if we delve into the topic .. Maybe you will change your mind .. Historical observations and stories about these creatures have been recorded from ancient times to the Middle Ages, especially in remote areas and in various parts of the world. Perhaps this abundance of narratives in terms of time, place, and multiple sources is what gave the theme a kind of realism away from the mythical world, or rather prompted researchers to unearth and find a realistic origin for the legend.

And let's start our exploratory journey from ancient times, how decapitated men were mentioned by (Headless men) by Herodotus in his history, talking about static people in ancient Libya, he claimed the presence of these creatures in the eastern part of the country along with other strange and ugly creatures such like people, dogs and wild jungle. In the same context, Pliny the Elder mentioned the Blemmi tribe in his natural history, counted them as tribes of North Africa and said: (They have no heads, and their mouths and eyes lie in their chests), and they say that these tribes live in Ethiopia.

The historian Strabo also mentioned them, saying that they are peaceful and live in the eastern desert near the city of Meroe in Sudan. In fact, there was already a tribe called Plims that lived in southern Egypt and participated in several wars against the Romans.

Belmia was not necessarily headless, as some authors have mentioned that they hid their heads between their shoulders. Perhaps this is more realistic, and perhaps the origin of the legend belongs to people with some kind of physical disability or moral deformation, such as a back strap that makes their heads hang over their chests. The French theologian Samuel Buchart touched upon this word (plimia) and said that it comes from two terms or two Hebrew words meaning "without a brain." This means that the Blimi people were people without brains.

In the Age of Exploration, English explorer and adventurer Sir Walter Raleigh spoke of a beheaded man named Ivipanuma when he spoke of his expedition to Guyana County in Venezuela. In fact, it was not so much an expedition as a journey in search of gold and ancient American treasures. Rally was determined that what he saw was real, but most likely he himself did not see these decapitated people, rather inspired his story from the stories of the American Indian tribes settling these places, and I also cite what some early Spanish travelers mentioned it in their books.

Dog People :

As for dogs, the Aztecs in Mexico absolutely believed in their existence, claiming that they were monsters who kill hunters, and they believed that these creatures, called Naguals, stole cheese and raped women, but did not kill anyone unless they were exposed to them. These creatures are truly magicians of people who are able to hide in various forms and bodies. These myths still resonate in some remote areas of Mexico, where people believe that Nguel are people who can transform into animal forms at night and use this ability to commit crimes, theft and rape, signifies almost the same idea of a werewolf in European folklore. ...

Transforming creatures have another example in Native American myths, especially Navajo folklore in the United States, where the cattle myth is whipped (skin walker) And it speaks of male and female evil witches who are able to transform and move in the form of animals, and the magician can get this extraordinary ability, by committing a disgusting act that destroys the human side of his personality and remains only on the side of animals, such as killing his family members or rape or sex with corpses in cemeteries - Nicrovelia - Far from America, the ancient world knew many myths about people with dog-headed, and most likely most of these myths come from the forms of ancient pharaonic deities, especially Anubis, the god of the dead incarnated in the form of a man with a jackal head, and also Xabi, one of the four sons of Horus guarding the throne of Osiris in the underworld, who appears like a baboon-headed man who looks like a dog, of course. Inspired by these ancient Egyptian myths, the myth of the people who were afflicted (Cynocephaly) appeared, and ancient Greek sources mentioned that these people are wild people who inhabit India and settle in the high mountains, and they said that these people or tribes communicate with each other other through the bark and live on the hunt. As for the famous historian Herodotus, he mentioned that they are among the people who settle in the eastern part of Old Libya, and we touched this nose. Many people in ancient times believed that these creatures did exist, and indeed they were real in terms of the fact that there was a long debate about whether they were descendants of Adam and Eve or not. He was believed to be super powerful and evil. Some ancient religious texts reported that they were violent people living in the city (human carnivores) and that the Lord sent apostles to them and that they entered Christianity and rejected their previous evil deeds. In this regard, we find several Christian Orthodox drawings depicting St. Christopher as a dog-headed man. Some ancient manuscripts said that Saint Christopher was originally a wild man with a dog's head living in the land of Canaan, eating human flesh and barking like dogs, but he regretted his actions and repented after he met Christ and he was rewarded for it is by returning to human nature and becoming his head like other people. Of course, this is only one of many stories about the life of St. Christopher. The most famous novel is that he was a natural person from the Canaanite people, but he was huge and had a terrible face.

The belief in the existence of human dogs continued into the Middle Ages in Europe, and it is possible that the legend of the wolfman was originally based on the legend of the dog.

The first European travelers, such as Giovanni and Markopou-lou, also mentioned dog stories. Giovanni said that the Mughal Emperor Oktay Khan fought wild dog-headed men in the north sea. As for Markopoulou, he mentioned that there is an island near China, inhabited by barbarians with their huge bodies and their heads in the form of dog heads.

One-eyed :

Other strange myths touched upon by ancient sources are those that spoke of one-eyed creatures, creatures that were very popu-lar among the Greeks and Romans, known as the Cyclops, and are said to belong to the same race as the giants.

The most famous stories and legends of the Cyclops are those that speak of polyphemus, and this was detailed in the Odessa epic of Homer, who was said to have lived with his people of giants on the island of Sicily and tended animals and ate human flesh led by their stumbling block on his island.

One of those who fell into the power of Polyphemus is the epic champion Odysseus and his twelve men. The giant locked them in his cave and closed the exit path with a large stone, then he ate two of them every day.

Odysseus and his people were thinking of a way to escape from the wild giant, and Odysseus had some wine, so he introduced him to the giant, who drank quickly and fell asleep, and be-fore going to bed, he looked at Odysseus and asked him for his name and promised to reward him if he will tell him the truth, and Odysseus said his name was "Nobody" The giant said that he would reward him by supporting him so that other people would not be eaten.

The giant fell into a deep sleep due to alcohol, and Odysseus prepared a large stick and worked hard to sharpen his head, and then sewed it into the sleeping giant's eyes, causing him to be blind, when his people heard this, they laughed and made him think. that he was crazy.

In the morning, the giant opened the cave door to take out his sheep and he lost his sight, which allowed Odysseus and his companions to escape after they tied themselves to the stomachs of the sheep, and as soon as they left the cave, they ran to their ship on the coast. , rode it and drove the creators from the island, while their boat sarcastically propelled Odysseus out of the giant Polyphemus, he told him that his real name was Odysseus and that he had deceived him, so he blew up Polyphemus with a cry, and due to the intensity of anger he tore out a large rock and threw it into the sea towards Odysseus's ship, and he would almost destroy the ship if not for the hand of fate that extended to save Odysseus and his companions.

Odysseus's story with the one-eyed giant Polyphemus is clearly reflected and echoed in the third Sinbad voyage at sea, how Sinbad and his companions landed an unknown island in the sea and were kept in a giant palace that eats people, and they fled just as Odysseus and his companions fled.

Greek mythology also tells us about three other giants of the Cyclops, who are the brothers Prontes, Strups and Argis, who were brothers of Titan, the first deities who ruled the world and were descendants of the Lord of the Earth and the God of Heaven, but a coup led by a young goddess led by Zeus removed the adult deities and sent them to a deep prison underground. Three siblings lined up with Zeus and they were very skilled at blacksmithing, so they made him a deadly weapon .. Lightning.

There is another legend about the one-eyed, and it talks about the sisters of Graia, and they are three sisters-witches who took turns looking with one eye, each of them waiting for their role to look at her and look at her.

Ancient historical sources also spoke of the existence of one-eyed peoples, one of which was said to have lived in southern Russia and was called Arimaspi, a Scythian tribe of powerful warriors and was in constant war with its neighbors. German folklore also features the terrifying warriors of Hagen. In Ireland, there is a giant Balor who dies instantly, anyone who dares to look at his one eye.

Arab and Islamic sources:

There have been many references to the presence of these strange peoples in the books of Arab and Muslim travelers and geography. The geographic sheikh, Al-Ottomani Al-Dai Mohiddin Ibn Muhammad Al-Rayes, who was 962 AH on his maps, stated that in South America: (The peoples of the people have their faces in chests, and they have no heads, and the length one of them is seven cubs, and his eyes are an inch and they are harmless, and other peoples have fox and dog faces),.

Zakariya Al-Quzaini said in his book the book (Wonders of creatures and the strangeness of assets) In the department - strange nations - he said about them - nation (Minsk) On the other hand, they have ears like elephant ears, and each ear looks like clothes (They are tall and wide) - And among them is a nation on the islands of the sea with faces like the faces of dogs and their whole body, like the body of people, they feed on the fruits of trees, and if they find something from the animals that they ate, including a nation that does not have a head for their bodies, mouths and eyes on their breasts)

This was mentioned in the book (greatness) The father of Sheikh Abdullah ibn Muhammad al-Eshbani, spoke about these nations, where he said with long support, quoting a man from the people of Rumia: (A man came up to us with a trace of scratches, So we asked: what is it on your face ?? He said: we went out on a boat, The wind blew on the island, We could not leave, The people of their faces brought us the faces of dogs, And their whole creation looks like the creation of people, The man of them preceded us, Others stopped us, So the man took us to his home, If he is wide and has a measure of copper on his furniture, Around him are skulls, weapons and a market of people! So we entered the house, and if there was a man who hit him like that, what happened to us, then he made us bring food and fruits, and this man told me: rather, this food will feed you, so who of you will eat it! So look at yourself, like my friends. He said: I was below food! So everyone who was fat of my friends went with this and ate this, So this man and I stayed Look, He attended their feast, And the man said to me: Prepare a feast for them so that they go to all of them, They remain three, If you survive, then, As for me, my people go, I know that this is the fastest thing to ask, And I breathe in the smell, I know the effect of man, Except for those who entered under such a tree, And the tree abounds in their country. So I went out a night prisoner, And the day lay under a tree, And when it was the third day, if they came like dogs, they would cut my archeology, They passed this tree while I was on it, The effect was cut off from them, And they came back, When they passed, I believed and went out, So I walk this island when he raised a big tree for me, I finished it, So there are all fruit trees, And if under his shadow men, as good as I saw Andy's image of men, So I went to the club of them, I made them talk, so they don't understand my words, I don't understand their words, So I sat with them like a man put his hand on me, So it's on my neck, Then he sprained my legs, Then get up, So I made him suffer .. Simply put, it was scratched on my face and made me turn on these fruits so that they would reap them and throw them to the owners and they laughed! When I passed out, I cut it into grapes, then I snapped it in the rock, squeezed it and left it, even if it boiled in it, He said: what is it ?? So I said, I'm in a hurry, So he parted and got drunk, His legs were broken, I dropped it, I went out until I pushed into the city, When I fell off it, if people like trees, Most of them are uneven, Ali met a group that led me to her prince, He ordered me to be imprisoned, They ended up locked up like a chicken cage, When they entered me, I broke it, They neglected me, I lived in them. Then, if they are preparing for battle, then I told them: what is this? They said: the enemy is coming to us, so we went to bed soon, and if the most naked, then I took a stick, and I stressed it, so I flew and went about them, so they honored me and glorified me, so they missed by women, and they said: we are married to you! Whenever my husband married a woman, she would kill her! They said: stay with us and don't mind killing them! So I went to two chests and I took them from the bark of the trees, then I tied magazines and I put food and water in them and I set and convinced the rest of the dress with me, so the wind threw me at you ..! ! These are bats from what I told you).

This island was also mentioned by Ibn Al-Wardi in the book of Harida Al-Ajabaa and Farida Al-Gharib, and he said as Abu Sheikh Al-Asbani spoke about it in some (Ottoman documents) indicating the existence of these peoples. ,. As Ibn Ayas al-Khanfi noted in The Flower of Flowers, the news about the peoples who live on the sixth earth below us, so he mentioned among them the nation with human bodies and dog heads! ...

The news of these peoples without the heads of their bodies was also mentioned in the book (Knowledge) And he said: (Then the king of the disciples ruled servant ben Abraha, and he panicked, he was so called because he invaded the land of the people of Nesnas and he killed a great death from them, and he returned to Yemen from their captivity with people of their faces in their chests) He is twenty-five years old),.

The origin of these myths

In fact, scientists have yet to find people with faces in chests, people with a dog's head, or giants with one eye. But believers in stories beyond nature and strangeness provide some explanations for these stories, saying that there is no smoke without fire, and that the ancients would not unanimously mention these myths if they did not have a realistic origin. Some of them went on to say that these people existed, but they died out due to the expansion of people, and this is actually an accusation that we cannot remove people due to the tendency towards aggression and violence that they have known throughout their history. ...

And there are those who see these people are wavy and wavy and they are imprisoned for the rest of the day.

While others see them as people with a hollow earth, a topic that has been talked about for a long time.

As far as scientific explanations go, most of these myths are due to rare human handicaps and disabilities, as we have said, it is most likely that the rear camera is the source of the myth of the decapitated people, while humans are dogs. There are people who grow out their hair profusely, completely covering their faces and bodies so that people think they are wolves or dogs (this is due to a rare genetic defect that causes a condition called congenital hyper hair (hypertrichosis). Of course, the ancients are nothing knew about genes, so they probably considered a person with these diseases from a group of monsters. As for people of one eye, it is said that the origin of the legend comes from the look of blacksmiths in ancient times. These people covered one of the eyes with skin and worked with only one eye and the reason for this is that the blacksmith realized that blindness was his inevitable fate as a result of his long look at the fire, which he uses in his work to melt, knock, and adapt iron, for this he only used one eye, to work while the other eye covered it and kept it intact for its retirement !.

LEGACY AND MEMORIES WITH THE IMPOSSIBLE

The happiest moments of my childhood are those moments when I put my head on the chest of my beloved mother to tell me a story before going to bed.I only listen to her sweet voice, which falls, and its tone rises in accordance with the events of the story until it will become a faint whisper, thinking that I have fallen asleep, and when accused of sneaking out of my area, he grabbed her by the clothes to crave more, and who among us did not crave? ...

She threatened me with her unforgettable finger, saying: (Sleepy, aka the father of the man who was stolen and the ghouls will come to eat you) This phrase will make my eyes sleep, leaving me, horror and obsessions third! There are many questions in my little mind that are mixed with moans

- What if the ghoul came while I was still awake? - I will play the role of the sleeper. - But he will find out, he is not stupid. - How will he know? - When your bed gets wet, clumsy! - So I will sleep quickly, otherwise he will come and devour me immediately, and he will not leave me, except on the condition of my red hair, because they will stand in his throat, and he will not be able to swallow them (the mind of children) I wish I could turn to a hairy bond to survive this miserable fate! ...

At the time, I didn't think that the adults who always forbade us to lie were also lying, even if their intention was good! ...

I found that the ghoul that froze with the blood from my veins, clung to me and inhabited my bed, the stillness of the dead is nothing more than an object of previous imagination, mentioned in popular scary stories to intimidate and intimidate cowards like me! ...

But or not all myths have even a small percentage of truth? The ancients built it and built the building until it became a myth of excessive intimidation and exaggeration! ...

The poet says that in the past Ghul was considered impossible for the Arabs

When I saw the children of time and what was in them *** vinegar and in trouble, I learned that the impossible three *** ghouls, the phoenix and the sure vinegar

And our article today will be subject to these impossible.

Ghoul:

A mythical creature in the form of a human, but its legs are don-key's legs, and thank God that this time we rested the legs of the goats when we borrowed them and weighed them to glue them to every blurry object in front of us! ... His eyes are cut to length, filled with anger and sparks, and a jaw with enormous fangs that can rip apart the bodies of his victims and turn them into the fin-gers of a sweater that is easy to swallow and digest.

The ghouls in the Arabs are a kind of apostasy of the jinn who lie in wait for travelers in the deserts and Fiavi, ridicule them until they are lost, and eventually settle in their steel belly.

And the female ghouls is a cough, and she is a demonic creature that covers her body with thick hair, but she is able to transform into the form of Eve girls, especially beautiful ones who live in abandoned places and what a difficult moment to throw fate in his path (His mother calls him) You seduce him until he takes his will, then fuck him, and before he wakes up from his ecstasy, he turns into a grip in her throat! ...

In my beloved country, Egypt, these characteristics are similar to that of a woman, often referred to by grandmothers in their stories, which is a "flutter" that attracts men with its softness, warm voice, calling them by name until they charm them and they go to two levels that do not have a third .. Either death or madness! ...

And there is a famous Egyptian movie called The End, one of its songs reads: (Something from afar called me, and the first thing that Grali called me was my neighbor).

And killing a cough is only one way, and he stabbed his shadow with a sharp blade.

And ghouls in some African cultures call a kind of activation, similar to the legendary "cyclopedia". This object, which was mentioned in the epic Odyssey when the Odysseon hero and his men were captured by a giant with one eye visible in the middle of his forehead called the Cyclops, is known for its gluttony. There is human flesh, but in the end they managed to escape from the fist.

And there are some heritage books that indicate that the ghoul is nothing more than a giant snake known as a ghoul and a type of snake known for the bay.

And I leave you, dear reader, to choose the ghoul that suits your imagination.

Phoenix:

The greatest bird of fire, a symbol of life and death, the optimal embodiment of the doctrine of eternity and resurrection among the pharaohs, for a person will rise after death to live forever, and his soul will ascend to heaven, because death was not the end, but rather the gateway to eternal life, as it happens in the legend of the phoenix.

As for the word "Phoenix", some say it is of Greek origin, while others say the word "Phoenix" as this bird was a symbol of the great Phoenician civilization in ancient Syria and painted its structure on its ships that roamed the seas.

As for the Arabs, it was called "Phoenix" because of the length of its neck, and the Arab world "David Al-Antaki" described it as: (The size of the camel is close, and the neck is lifted from it for a long time, very white, surrounded by zero).

Some have confused it with the rookie bird, which is the giant bird of the Akban family. Ibn Battuta mentioned this on one of his trips, saying: (And when the forty-third day appeared to us after dawn, a mountain in the sea between us and twenty miles between it and the wind carried us to it, the sailors were surprised and said: we are not on land , and there is no covenant in the sea, mountains, so people resorted to forgiveness and entreaty, and the wind calmed some immobility, Then we saw that mountain when the sun rose, and it rose into the air, and there was a light that we imagined, there was a mountain which is nothing more than a beginner) Dear Reader, can you imagine the size of this bird, which was hiding the sunlight from this distance! ... And there is the legend of the Phoenix, the legend that the long-lived phoenix comes every five hundred years, at the end of that and when he feels that his age is moving towards the Temple of the Sun in Egypt, his wings slide down and they contain bubbles of "white phosphorus" which ignites immediately after it combines with air.It then turns the bird into a fireball of fire that appears on its feathers, flesh and bone, and only a handful of ash is left from this body, from which the worm soon turns into a cocoon, which emerges after a few days. The new phoenix is almost a mirror image of its predecessor, flying back to the original homeland to begin a new course.

And for Phoenix - the famous story with our master Solomon, when he entered his congregation and said: (I do not believe in fate, because this is a person who makes his own fate, not God).

Peace be upon him (the Creator of predestination is God, and man only needs to choose between good and evil) and his task is to change the fate of a poor girl who is going to be born in the north of the country and will marry one of the sons of the kings of the south in a place for outside the country! Although Phoenix stole the girl after her birth and placed her on a remote island, he could not prevent fate, Solomon punished him with exile in the mountains and did not allow him to mix with the rest of the birds, and it is said that since then no one has seen him.

The phoenix held a great place in ancient times that exceeded the position of the dragon, especially in ancient Chinese civilization. They were blessed with this super beautiful bird and one of their authors said this: (For rooster phoenix, snake neck, bird mouth, turtle and fish tail). Phoenix can be a legend or a fact that doesn't matter, it's important to learn a lesson from your legend and start over, when some think we are over, shake off the ashes and start a new day from which we forget the old one, and that's what the persistent did Gaza City, when took this bird logo for her, they both rise again in the ashes.

condom: Is loyal vinegar impossible to exist like a ghoul and a phoenix? The vinegar that loves you and befriends you without a goal, is afraid of you even from the surface of himself, a person, as if he is a part of you, as if your heart is his heart, and as if your mind is his mind, two bodies separate and share one soul, the person who takes the sadness away from you before you drown in it, the person if you make a mistake, accepts your excuses and if you're just protecting your secrets, has this person become a form of imagination after most human relationships turned into a relationship of interests that disappear with the disappearance of purpose and purpose? ! It has become a physical relationship defined by numbers, it has a stake in the exchange of life, just like an oil well that everyone flows into until its springs dry up.

Winston Churchill described the friendship by saying: (She is looking for a black cat in a blind man's black room) .. Like her decision and very dark Winston! ...

Friendship like watermelon can make you happy, be red, delicious, and your luck can be against you, and the choice is more delicious! And you won't know the type of watermelon except during disasters, because it is the only one that shows your friend's metal and masks falling off their faces. And there is an Egyptian proverb that says: (As in the anti-bark shampoo in the Sahaba against ten).

LEGENDARY CREATURES AND CREATURES

Aliens:

Many people said they saw it, but there is no evidence, and many people said that it will come one day and take the land, and it may be nice and not occupy it, but just visit this, and many films, stories and myths have arisen. although the spread of these stories that say they are on earth is a myth that was invented by the wider human mind, and this is from his imagination, nothing more, nothing less, and with the development of man and his arrival on the moon and into space, why they did not find aliens, they hid or ran away, fearing for their lives, or they did not live in space, and many questions were asked by people, and yet man did not find an answer to them? Space is real or not, and on this site we have touched on alien abductions by people for analysis, understanding of their type and ability to live.

It is also said that in the past, aliens occupied the Earth, but died from germs and microbes that could not be tolerated by humans in the future. When science and machines develop, we will surely know what the truth of their existence is.

Butterfly:

The legend of a man with red eyes and two large wings and his clothes are black, that he can fly and reports increased in 1966 and 1967 in West Virginia, and some who saw him said that sometimes he had no head with only his body and his red, eyes were in his chest, and he was last seen on the bridge of the Silver Bridge. Then the bridge fell, and in 1967 it killed 46 people.

And I think it might be there, but if I saw him headless, I would pass out from horror and fear of the horror of what I saw. If you want to know more about him, just write to the mouthpiece in any search engine.

Montek Monster:

People discovered that this animal was lying on the beach dirty in the sand of the beach in 2008 and when it was found it was dead on Montac Beach in New York and the picture spread around the world and it became an unknown creature and its body disappeared into the mysterious, circumstances and scientists could not research it and know its type.

I think it is a product of marrying a cow and a pig, and that explains the shape of the body. As for the face, I don't know because it has fangs and its nose is odd in color. As for how it disappeared, it's weird because of that, I doubted it was from aliens, but its shape is not alien related

Helicoprien:

It is considered a type of dinosaur 15 feet long, its lower jaw is twisted, and its teeth are many, numerous and very sharp, and scientists believe that it lives in the depths of the oceans and is called (Spiral Saw) Because its teeth resemble a saw and are one of the few creatures that survived for a while (Epoch of the Great Death) During this period, 99% of the mythical creatures ended, and some traces were found indicating their existence. There is no doubt that this creature has lived on our planet for millions of years, and its size ranges from 3 to 4 meters.

4 TERRIFYING JAPANESE MYTHS

Hon-una :

Hon-she, one of the Japanese urban myths, is considered a beautiful and beautiful woman in the morning, but at night Hong-she looks for her prey (men) when she looks for a man in dark alleys and streets, woe is the man you find .. Where she pounced on him and took him to her hut to do what she wanted.

There is another story for Hon-on. Hon_una is said to be a very pretty and beautiful woman who wears clothes that cover her entire body and only her neck and face emerge from it, but this beauty is only her assistant to seduce men, since then if she finds a man on a dark street that will seduce her with his beauty, a man will follow her wherever she goes from the seriousness of her beauty, After that she enters her house and then takes off her long clothes, then her body appears, and these are only bones. There is never meat, except in the neck and face! .. And as soon as a person sees this scene, Hun-she embraces him and begins to suck his soul and blood.

Hanko-san -

Hanko-san is one of the most famous ghost stories in Japan, and it tells the story of the ghost of a little girl who died during World War II. This ghost is always present in the third bathroom on the third floor in school buildings.

There are many stories about Hanko-san's ghost, but the most famous story is that when you enter the bathroom on the third floor of the girls' school, you go to the third bathroom and knock on the door three times, and then ask, "You are here, Hanko-san? ". The ghost girl will answer you, "I am here," and if you are encouraged and enter the bathroom, you will find a little girl in a white shirt and red skirt - a costume of clothing in Japan during World War II. -.

Most of Hanko-san's ghost stories seem peaceful, but there are also stories of frightening incidents that happened to those who dared to name a ghost. It is said that some of those who heard the girl's voice and entered the bathroom did not find her inside, but found a huge terrifying lesbian who ate them. There is a story that says that after summoning the ghost of Hanko-san, a white hand or a bloody hand appears, and the person demanding strength is pulled into the bathroom and no one sees her after that.

Cow head:

This is one of the scariest Japanese urban myths .. But at the same time, no one knows what is happening ..

Is it a mystery? .. How to be the scariest and at the same time nobody knows what is going on.! ..

Just because it's all about listening to the story (cow's head) according to legend, everyone who listens to the story doesn't go crazy or die after a short period of time, and for this reason there is no one to repeat the story, so we know what its content is. All we know is that the story is so horrible that nightmares, madness and death will catch up with everyone who listens to it.

What a strange legend ..

The most famous stories about this legend say that a Japanese teacher told scary stories to calm his students during the bus ride. Among the stories he told was the story of a cow's head, and as soon as he finished her novel, he passed out, the students started screaming, and the driver got so scared that his hands were sweating and began to shake, and the teacher is said to have died, in while the students have lost their memory! ...

Background Yuri:

Ghosts rise from the depths of the sea to attack ships ... This myth is about sea ghosts or the lives of people who drown in ship wrecks.

It is believed that these vengeful and evil spirits, due to their terrible death, rise from the depths of the sea to take the lives of sailors and fishermen in their ships and boats, soaring in the seas and rivers, as they want others to experience the same bitter path of death. which she tried when she died.

According to legend, everyone who makes these ghosts die also becomes one of them and participates in the pursuit of ships and sailors.

This myth is widespread among sailors, they believe in it and perform certain rituals to ward off the evil of these evil ghosts, such as throwing certain types of food and vows into the sea.

MYSTERIOUS WIZARD - SERIAL KILLER FROM THE EAST

A century ago, the inhabitants of the Arabian Peninsula for their lives depended on livestock of all kinds, and for them the capital on which their lives were based was food, drink, clothing and shelter, and animals were the only means of transportation and travel, and one of the most important tools for waging wars among them, some of them were also involved in the trade of these animals, especially beauty. It is transported to herds in neighboring countries such as Jordan and Egypt and sold there during certain seasons and on its own commercial travel.

At the beginning of the twentieth century, there was a person working in the field of beauty, where he buys it from his owners with a certain financial amount until he collects a large number of them, and then goes to Egypt, crossing Jordan and Palestine to sell it there, and from this man had an assistant from the islanders who worked to help him in his work and his commercial travels and to part on his return.

In one of the commercial transactions, if you can call it that, the merchant bought a group of camels, and then he and his assistant prepared for departure, prepared their trips and set them up, then they went to Egypt.

When they arrived in Egypt after months of travel, and this was during the reign of King Farouk, they were arrested by the Egyptian guard, where some police officers denounced so many camels and were suspicious of them, so two men were taken to investigate the matter. The police introduced them personally to King Farouk, based on the man's assistant's novel, and perhaps the procedures at the time were less costly and bureaucratic, Or that the assistant heard the name of King Farouk hesitating in the office, so he thought whoever would meet him was King Farouk when he was Chief of Police !.

King Farouk (or Chief of Police) asked them who they were and why they were accompanying this huge number of camels, so the merchant told him that he was a beauty merchant and had come to Egypt to sell him and return to where he came from. ,. Therefore, the king asked him about the reason for selling beauty in Egypt, condemning that the Egyptians ate camel meat, but the man confirmed this and said that this was not the first time he had sold beauty in Egypt and that the Egyptians were already eating camel meat. The king looked at one of his assistants standing around him and asked him if the Egyptians generally ate camel meat, so he confirmed his help, and that camel meat was one of the types of meat that the Egyptians eat.

After a simple, uncomplicated procedure, the two men were released, so the merchant sold the beauty, gave his assistant his share and told him to go his own way and return to his family, and the two men parted in Egypt, where the merchant was there, and his assistant returned to Arabian Peninsula.

On the way back to his family, after walking a long distance, he found a small plateau (It is believed that it is now known as the border between Saudi Arabia and Jordan) He wanted to rest in the delusion of this plateau, He descended from the end of his journey and began to prepare a place where he would rest, While he was busy with this, he heard a very strange sound, as if the earth trembled under him with this sound, And when he looked at the sound, he saw a huge snake, like you were black, coming out of one from the caves inside this plateau, and he went to the camel, so that the camel died immediately, and during this the man looked quiet, amazed at what was happening and did not lift a finger, after that the snake returned, The cave that came out of it and disappeared , the man examined his camel, who was counting his vehicles, and found him dead and motionless.When he learned that he would have to complete his journey, the barefoot man who skinned the dead camel skin was barked his shoes off him and brought them to the open air to dry so that he could wear them, after the shoes dried and broke through, during the march, the man collided with the donkey and the strange man greeted him and took them They say, then he asked him where he is from, so he told him about his trip to Egypt and his return from it, so he invited him to dine with him and rest before he completed his journey, so the man agreed to this and accompanied him to where he lives ...

The two men went to an old filthy house from houses of that time and had lunch.The strange man asked him to stand with him to show him the room in which he would rest before completing his travel itinerary.In good faith, he obeyed him and stood with him in that room, reassuringly. When he entered the room, another man closed the door behind him and closed it with a key, so the man surprised this and urged him to open the door for him, but he did not answer him, waiting for him to open the door, but the man disappeared.

He looked around the filthy room and found terrifying views of human skeletons, some old and some modern. He was very afraid of this scene, and during this he heard a strange sound, from which the columns of the room were trembling, and if a large black snake came out of one of the corners of the room, he opened his neck wide and crawled towards him, so when he approached him, he tried to bite him, but the man looked for it and left on the other side.

The man's shoes, which he made from camel skin, were stiff and became hard and sharp like an ax because he did not tan the skin, so he took it off his foot and grabbed it to avoid the snake, and used it as a weapon, rescue , and in the next attack of the snake he received a beating in front of the shoe and stabbed her with it, so he died immediately, the man stayed, he looks tense from the situation, I'm waiting for what will happen next, but there is stillness in the room.

The man was left in a room with a dead snake and skeletons, and he sat waiting, not knowing what would happen to him and what he could do. He remained in this state for three days. Suddenly, the door of the room was opened and the man entered, but he was surprised that he was still alive, looked at the dead snake and enlarged, It surprised him and asked how he could kill him, So he told him about the shoes that he made of the skin of a camel, which was bitten by a snake, and he said to him, "I want you to take me to the place where the accident happened." And since the man was weak, exhausted of strength and will, He did not eat for three days, obey human order without resistance.

The strange man prepared two trips for each of them, and he set it up and headed to the plateau where the camel died when they arrived there, the body of the camel when the owner left it and it started to decompose, the strange man showed a box full of butter, and told the person: "I want you to paint oil all over my body, not, She goes anywhere without covering it with oil. "He took off his clothes and gave the oil jar to the man, so he did what he was asked to do, but while he applied the oil to his back, he left part of his back open without applying it or feeling it. ,.

After that, the man stood, and the oil covered his body, closed his eyes, and began to read the incomprehensible magic talismans, And when he finished his talismans, a very strange sound and terrifying rustle appeared from a cave, small in the mountains, and his echo shook him, therefore he came out of the cave as a huge black snake and headed towards the charming man until he reached his feet, so he began to climb up on him, wrapping himself around his body and heading towards his head, but when He reached the place in the back that the man had left without applying his to butter. He bit him in this place, then began to turn around strongly and press his ribs until the person heard them crushing, and continued until he fell down dead, so the snake returned to its cave from which it came out and the ground was shocked with the right sound.

All this, and the person looks at these amazing strange events, not knowing what happened, and at the same time wondering at the strangeness of this butcher and the reason why he commits these crimes? And the heaps of skeletons from his victims in the filthy room who kidnapped and tricked them to kill them? And why collect snakes, kill their travelers and cross the road?

All these questions could never be answered, and when the scene ended and the magician died and the snake returned to his cave, he accepted two offers, riding one and leading the other, and completed his journey to his family in a safe and secure manner.

ROVA AND THE BEAST .. THE LEGEND OF AVE INOV

In ancient times, hundreds of centuries ago, when the world was full of supernatural events and miracles, animals laughed, cried and talked with a person .. In one area of the world, in particular in the village of Amazig, there was a family of six people, a father and four children, and a very beautiful girl named Rova (strange). All the boys were brave and tough and inherited their physical strength from their father (Enova), who could kill a powerful bull with one blow of his fist. This family was afraid and respected everyone, Rova is the eldest and spoiled daughter among her brothers, everyone saves her with his own life so that no one touches her with misfortune. They each had wonderful and distinctive abilities for him, for example, an older brother can make land and seas and his next brother can see through walls, then the younger has a supernatural hearing that allows him to hear dew drops, while the fourth and the last one is smart With skill and ease, he can steal eggs from a partridge while she hugs them without feeling it.

In the traditions and customs of that ancient time, members of the tribe were cooperative and synergistic with each other, always meeting every night in a huge forest located under the village to exchange conversation and comment on the events of their day and solve their problems and conflicts, they also had different books and legal constitutions for sure About the laws of our time, but they still had enough justice and common sense to please everyone with all kindness and peace.

When they were talking one night, they heard a terrible sound accompanied by a stench, so they took out their weapons

To prepare to fight this creature that awaits them, but he soon disappeared from sight before they caught him, so the residents suggested building a muddy hut in which they lay down their weapons and protect it from weather and predators, as well as from of this ghoul roaming around, so they gave a guard mission to Rova's father. He became the one who leads this place and remains in it day and night, and his daughter Rova prepares food for him every day and brings him twice, once at noon and once at night.

The doors did not have locks, as now, so Enova put a large filling near the door so that no one would sneak into it, and he agreed with his daughter to enter the password, where he first asks her: "Who are you?" She says: "Imagine Eldi Taporta Ava Inova. "I mean, open the door for me, Daddy Inova, I am your daughter Rova." Then she squeezes her silver bracelets until he hears her voice and is sure that it is.

One day a ghoul secretly approached the hut and stole a rumor to find out the words between Rova and her father, and so he took the right opportunity, stood near the door and said: "Open the door for me, Daddy Inova, I am your daughter Rova." And the father knew that it was not the voice of his daughter, although Gul had a voice similar to the voices of people, and he told him: "Get out of here, you are not my daughter Rova. I do not open the door to anyone, your voice is different, and I did not hear your bracelets. " And the next day, when Rova came, her father did not dare to open the door for her until he asked her to repeat her words several times, until he was convinced that she was there, and told her that the ghoul was trying to imitate her.

After several unsuccessful attempts, Ghul decided to consult with Amgar (a wise old man)

And he went up to him and said to him: "I have a sore throat. Please give me a prescription for treatment. I want my voice to become very soft, like the voice of a young girl, I beg you .. And I also want to have something that sounds like bracelets to entertain little children. ". Al-Hakim replied, "Well, that's easy .. As for your vote, there is only one solution. You have to fill your throat with sheep fat, then go to the ant's nest and open your mouth and let the ants enter. They will eat all the fat that surrounds your vocal cords, and therefore you will have a soft voice, like a child's .. As for the sound of the bracelets, it's very simple. Go to the river and take the shells of the empty shells, then make a contract with them and put them around your neck. When you move them, they will release nice and fun rattles for everyone.

He thanked the wise ghoul very much and went quickly to apply whatever he advised, roam in search of the ant's nest and repeat the experiment with thousands of ants until his voice was exactly the same as that of a little girl and looked for better shells until got the same sound as the Rova bracelets, then he went (Run to the hut and said the same secret phrase, and the father replied: (Chen Chen Tizwkatinim from A to Rova) This means that he wanted to hear the sound of the bracelets, and the ghoul moved necklace, and his stunt ended in complete success.

Inova opened the door, and he was surprised when he found, instead of his daughter, a terrible ghoul with big fangs preparing to pounce on him, looking at him with terrible eyes and saying to him: "And finally I caught you, where you want to start with the accusation, with head or feet? "Think carefully about the ghoul and decide to start with the feet so that the person could not resist and escape, and he began to destroy the poor body until he almost finished it .. And only a few minutes later a young woman, Rova, came and screamed in horror when she noticed that the door was wide open, but she did not run away, but decided to go in and ensure the safety of her father. He almost passed out from what she saw and the poor woman had no choice but to try to escape and warn the villagers, but after just a few steps, this monster grabbed her using his long strands of hair and then took her to his lair and placed in the room where he kept his food.

Rova started screaming loudly, asking for help from her terrible fate, waiting for her until her screams came

To the ears of her third brother, who has the ability to hear, he told his brothers: "Something bad is happening with our sister Rova, so let's move quickly to save her, it's not her habit of staying away this late evening. ,. ". They all ran to the hut and found in it only the blood and bones of their father. The third brother followed Rova's screams until they reached the dark den that was present in the wide and intimidating cave, and they discovered that it was tied to her wrists and legs by the strong tufts of Buzz's hair. Rova felt happy because she found her brothers safe and then burst into tears and said that the ghoul wanted to marry her and found no way to dodge him, so her brothers assured her that she would be safe and avenge their death father.

Rova remained in her place until Gul came and dragged him to him, he was very tired and tired of chasing prey all day, and he threw himself on the bed next to Rova. As soon as he fell into a deep sleep, the discerning brother used his talent to see what was behind the wall, so he told his brothers that it was time to save their sister, and so their brother, who had lightness, entered and brilliantly managed to weaken these tangled shackles from his sister's hands and left everyone as quickly as possible. They even walked away from this place and then sat down to rest for a while, but before they could catch their breath, their brother warned them that he heard Gulya's footsteps coming towards them.

Here the elder brother entered and managed with his amazing strength to dig a deep tunnel into the ground, then they all hid in it until, when the ghoul came, he began to say to himself: "I smell human flesh, but I don't see anyone !!" .. Ideas began to clash in his mind with questions and confusion, so he decided to stop searching, and then they left.

So after months of preparation and planning, the four brothers managed to get revenge on their father's killer using their intellect, talents and the power of their determination, so they returned safety and peace to their clan, and once they returned to their village until the villagers met them with great joy, celebrating and rejoicing in their great victory and two witnesses of Their great heroism.

EMILZIL IS THE LAND OF LOVERS .. LEGEND OF ISLI AND TESLA

"And out of love what was killed" is an old phrase that lovers spread among themselves, and it also hesitated on the lips of those who inherit the state of lovers or mock them in the same way .. But for the legend of Isli and Tesla, this is the perfect phrase for a wide love story that tied two young people from two rival tribes .. Kai Khabibin, whom he most wanted, had to live together under the roof of one house, but the conditions were stronger than them .. Thus, the two lovers chose another more tragic path to date of the birth of the greatest and most famous love story known to Berbers in extreme Morocco.

Lake Isle and Teslet .. Forbidden Love Code

The details of the legend relate to a love story involving a young man named "Moha" from the Eish Ibrahim tribe and a beautiful young woman named "Khada" from the Et Eza tribe, two Amazigh tribes located in a rugged mountainous region called "Machel" in the heart of the Great Atlas Mountains in southeast Morocco .. These two tribes are the main branches of the Berber Asigian tribes "White Hadidu" ..

He knew about the two tribes and their ancient feud, so the essence of their dispute centered on pastures and water, until the degree of disagreement reached the point of preventing marriage between them. But the two lovers did not lose hope and struggled to fulfill their dream of marriage, but their attempts were unsuccessful in the face of the intransigence of the two tribes and the escalation of hostility between them. Although the righteous "Sir Ahmed Omgani", before crowning their love and blessing, he was one of the experts and people known for his sobriety and wisdom .. However, the culture of hatred and hatred was much stronger than the culture of love. The two lovers were nothing more than a scar from misfortune, and they began to cry bitterly, and their eyes fell in heavy tears .. The boy's tears become a big lake, and his name is Isli, which in Arabic means "groom", and the girl's tears are small Lake Teslet (bride)

Emil season.. Coronation for lovers and redemption for separated lovers

This influential event prompted the Ait Hadidou tribes to pledge not to confront the lovers and to foster their rapprochement through group marriage, now known as the engagement season, which takes place between September 19th and 21st each year. , .. This season is the strangest holiday for lovers and the most famous in the world .. It attracts all lovers from various tribes of Ait Hadidu and beyond to get married in this place, which witnessed the suicide of two young people for her eternal love .. This is the season that crowns lovers and tempts the guilt of separating two lovers who have been united by love and separated by war. Today, according to the custom of the Ait Hadidu tribes, the girl is not forced to marry, nor is he married, except for love and the one who chooses her for my consent.

LOVELY LEGEND AND MONSTER

Once upon a time there was a simple old man who lived in a rural area in a simple hut and had three daughters. The little girl's name was Jamila, and she is one of the most beautiful women in her village, distinguished by intelligence, tenderness and tenderness, and she knew about her love for reading and books, so she was her first love, which she did not refuse.

One day, the old man told his daughters that he would go on a business trip, And tell them that each of them can request a gift, Immediately, the older girl decided to bring her a gold necklace, As for the middle girl, she wanted a precious dress, As for Jamila, she hesitated She knew that her father had a simple job and she could not bring many expensive things. I asked him for a soft red rose that would not cost him much.

The old father went on a journey and did his job, On the way back, she remembered the beautiful request of his daughter, He looked for a red rose a lot and did not find it, Then he passed a large abandoned palace, The palace was dark and frightening, But his garden is filled with all kinds of flowers While he was walking in the park, the father found a red rose for his lovely daughter, But when he picked it up, he surprised him by walking into a large monster in the garden, The Monster asked him why is he here? .. The father told him that he could not refuse his daughter's request, and she only asked him for a red rose, and he looked for it everywhere and found it here. The beast was angry and said that the price of choosing a rose without permission was to bring his daughter, who asked the rose to live with him in his gloomy palace.

The father returned to his house sad and gloomy, and when his daughter Jamila accepted him, she told him what was wrong with you, dad .. Why are you sad? ? .. He told her about this and said that if you do not go with me to this fateful palace, the monster will kill me, but I will never sacrifice you, I would rather kill me than take you away from me.

But Jamila rejected her father's words and asked him to take her to the Palace of the Beast to live with him, and when they taught her brothers this matter and rebuked her for this ridiculous request that cost her her life. But Jamila insisted on going.

When the father and daughter approached the Palace of the Beast, I heard him roar, and I was very scared, and I thought it was his roar .. How will it look? .. But she kept her fear and was silent so as not to sacrifice her father, because his sisters needed him.

When I entered the palace, I was surprised by a monster whose terror is in the heart of everyone who sees him, and he hides the upper part of his face with an ugly black cloak that wraps his whole body inward, and his hands are covered with thick hair, and his fingers are on it - sharp claws that tremble from them.

Despite her horror, Jamila asked her father to leave quietly. The amazed father left, leaving his daughter to an unknown fate. The castle closed its doors to that mysterious fate awaiting her with this monster, whom she married to the rose that her father had chosen for her. And if the case ended at that moment, the monster refused to speak to her and abuse her, he refused to illuminate the lights so that she would not see his face, which causes terror in the heart of every person.

And the beast coped with the beautiful torture, because he knows that he did not come to his palace for the love of him or for the desire of those in it, but rather came to protect her father and sisters, because her father chose this pathetic rose.

Over time, Jamila discovers that there is something abnormal in this palace, as all the freezers talk to her and gradually fall in love with this beautiful country girl. And gradually Jamila got used to living in this castle, and she even loved her, and she began to clean the palace, arranging it and coordinating flowers in its gardens. She brought life to these wild ruins with her beautiful, vibrant, elegant taste and sweet voice that captures the heart of everyone who hears her.

Jamila's only daily encounter with the castle monster was at the dinner table and the darkness hid the ugly monster's face, it was not beautiful that you could see well, but hearing his voice silently eating food. She has repeatedly tried to break the silence between them, so she talks to him, but every time he blocks it and tells her to shut up. However, she did not give up. She wanted to know why the monster mistreated her, why she was captured in this castle and why she deserved all this torture because of the rose that her father had chosen from his garden. Then the beast roars with a voice like thunder and lights up lightning in its eyes and shouts: "Do you think I'm a fool ??" .. I don't know what you and your father are hiding for me. ... Your father told me that you are going to marry a young man in your village, an arrogant man called "Gaston", and I hate you and I hate him.

Jamila was struck by the words of the beast, which he said with great hatred and hatred towards her, and began to cry in pain and try to tell him that the arrogant "Gaston" is the one who told the villagers that he would marry her, but she had not the slightest feeling, and all her interest was in books and reading. But the beast did not listen to her, because hatred and nervousness dominated him, so he interrupted her with his frightening voice, saying: "Don't try to trick me or even call me, we have nothing to say." Jamila silently went to her room, crying in pain because she didn't deserve it, so what is her fault ?? ..

While she was crying, her friends went to the freezers, tried to ease her grief, and began to sing to drive her sadness into her.

And her friends really excel at inanimate objects, taking them off the sadness in which they are, and when she looked at the things around her, hope entered her heart again and began to sing with them. Then the beast listened to his sweet voice, the voices of inanimate objects came, and they began to dance around Jamila, and they went all over the palace to sing, dance and ink.

When the monster was in his room, he seemed to feel a new feeling, in which he was a beast that had no feelings, He began to listen to the singing with interest and passion, He made his way on a limb outside his room to see life again comes to his palace as before, When she saw a beautiful monster, she reached out and pushed him to sing along with her, The monster held out his hand, which ends with sharp claws and thick hair, touching his grace, the beauty of her hand, and the beast felt a strange feeling, For the first time he feels it, I feel that I heard a lot about him .. This is "tenderness" that he did not taste .. And he began to sing in a low voice, in a rough tone, and he returned to silence, ashamed of the ugliness of his voice. As for Jamila, she began to cheer him up with a smile, and then their relationship took another turn and the monster began to love Jamila and learned the meaning of hope, love and optimism for the first time and began to emerge from its isolation day after day. He began to communicate with hand-some, but with a long robe, so that you will not see his ugly face until the day comes when I enter the darkness, an isolated room that was dedicated to a monster, and he entered it from time to time and spent long hours, howling in pain and sadness and going out, hating everything around him. She was beautiful, thought a lot about this room to find out what was in it and the curi-osity that controlled her pushed her to enter it, so she checked the room and saw a very beautiful red rose that you have not seen more beautiful than in glass box, then he entered the mon-ster, grabbed the rose and said, "Why did you catch my flower ?, thief? .. Get out of my palace, I don't want you. ".

She said: "I didn't mean it, I'm sorry."

He shouted to her: "Get out."

She left the palace sad, rode a horse and went, When she was half-way there she was surprised by the many wolves coming to her, and she was afraid, When the wolves approached her, she closed her eyes and breathed for the last time, When she opened eyes, she was surprised by a huge man with a black cloak all night, so she knew she was a monster, And the wolves fought for her, He went to her, hugged her, took her home and laid her on the bed, She slept deeply and woke up only then when the sun rose from the window of the room. She remembered the monster, so she went up to him and found that he was bleeding, fever, and he told her: "Go away."

And she said in the loudest voice: "I will not go, I will help you, whether you like it or not." Then I wiped off his blood, looked at him and took his forehead, and he turned into a human, so I asked him: "Who are you ??".

He said: "I am a beast."

She said, "How did you become a human?"

He told her that there was an evil, charming old man who had cast a spell on him and he turned him into a monster, and that he would not return to become human again unless the girl she loved accepted him with all his heart.

When I left his room with the monster, I was surprised by the people, so I asked them: "Who are you?"

They said: "We are inanimate objects and now we are back to normal after the curse is lifted from the palace."

And the beast said to Jamila: "I love you with all my heart, with my beauty .. will you marry me? ? ".

And she said to him: "Yes."

Then they had a very big party and the beauty invited her father and two sisters to her wedding, so they came and the beautiful woman married a monster and lived happily ever after.

***

The meaning of the story: from this story we learn that beauty is not the beauty of the form, but the beauty of the soul, because the monster was ugly, but beautiful, admired his spirit and loved him. Please do not blame you for appearing again, because they will disappear, but the soul will remain.

The Legend of Belle and the Beast is an ancient European heritage. It first appeared in a book in eighteenth century France, and since then has spread and famed throughout the world. There are many cited films, the most famous and successful, like the 1991 Walt Disney animated film Beauty and the Beast.

TRUE CLOWN

The clown is our pleasure in our childhood ... During circus shows ... Successful parties ... Birthdays.

He is an artist who performs comedy and wears makeup in strange clothes and unusual shoes. He goes to the theater to laugh at the audience, to play children, to perform with shows and games of ease.

But what does the legend say ??

The clown is basically an evil person who lives in a cave isolated from the American village, kidnaps and devours children in winter!..

His skin is white from cold weather, his nose is red from cold.

But this was not the only reason for the fear of clowns. There is a type of phobia called fear of clowns (courophobia)..

In fact, many people are afraid of artists who spend a lot of powders and cosmetics, and therefore people have been afraid of clowns for centuries . There is also an ancient legacy of the fear of clowns, Its roots may go back to the Middle Ages, We have all heard about the legend of the magic oboe (We wrote about this in detail on the website), It tells about the clown with the magic oboe who kidnapped all the children in the German city of Hamelen to avenge his family that ate his right, It is said that no one has seen the children after them, and their influence is gone forever.

As for our modern era, the most common fear of clowns is the famous American mobster John Wayne Jesse, who was known as the butcher's clown, He raped over 33 boys and teenagers and then horribly killed them and buried them under his house, His crimes and discoveries caused the wave of terror in the United States and distorted the image of the clown in an unprecedented manner. Contrary to rumors, John Jesse did not lure or kidnap boys in a clown costume, in fact he only wore a clown costume a few times, attending children's charity parties where he invented the character of a clown named Buggy for himself. ,. Honestly, his clown form is terrifying, and his gruesome sadistic crimes are even worse.

There is also a very popular folk tale in America that scared the clowns..

The story goes that a rich couple decided to spend an evening outside, They had a big house and two lovely children, a boy and a girl, The couple brought a nanny, She is a teenage girl who knows her well and trusts her, Before they leave home, tell me girl to take good care of the two children and prepare them for dinner, then send them to the family. After sleeping, she can sit and watch TV awaiting their return. The husband asked her to watch TV in their bedroom to be near the children's room in case they woke up at night, because they had nightmares in the last period, and the girl willingly agreed. That's right, the couple left for the evening while the girl stayed with her two children while they were awake.When she was sleeping, she went to the couple's bedroom and turned on the TV, But she turned her attention to the presence of a large clown statue standing in the corner of the room, What- what she didn't like about the statue, His eyes looked scary in the dark, As if he was watching her and following her movements, The girl tried to ignore the statue and was busy watching TV, But she could not, Her eyes involuntarily moved and looked at the statue , She had a strong sense of discomfort, She even imagined that he was moving, Very little, The more she turns her face, the better his position .. Or so I was deceived by fear.

Finally the girl could no longer sit there, she went to the first floor and called the couple on the phone ..

Girl: Hi .. Hi, it's me .. Don't worry, everything is fine and the kids are sleeping quietly in their beds .. I just called to ask if I could watch TV in the lobby instead of the bedroom.

Wife: Of course, dear, you can ... but why? ..

Girl: I know what I'm saying may sound stupid .. But I honestly feel a little fear of the clown statue ..

Wife: a clown statue ?! ..

Girl: Yes, a clown statue in your bedroom.

Wife: Wait a minute dear ..

Silence reigned for a while, then the girl heard her husband talking to her, and his tone was very disturbing and very serious ..

Husband: Listen well .. Now I immediately want you to go to the children's bedroom, pick them up from the family and quickly leave the house, and we will immediately call the police .. come on quickly ..

The girl trembles: But what's wrong? .. What is going on, please tell me? ..

Husband: We don't have a clown statue! ..

For a moment, the girl felt that her whole body felt raised up with fear, and a cold thing flowed from her head to the sole of her foot, But she grabbed and ran to the children's room, hugging them and chasing them out, When she went down the stairs, she turned behind and saw a clown standing up the stairs looking at her, and her heart almost stopped because of her, When I got to the bottom of the stairs, I looked again and saw the clown disappear into the darkness of the upper floor. The girl took her two children outside and took refuge in a neighbors house. A few minutes later the police came and searched the house. They found a clown hiding in the attic and they arrested him, They found a knife with him, He turned out to be a mentally ill man and a serial killer wanted by the police for several murders, And he hid in a couple's house for months, He hides in the attic during the day and when the couple sleeps at night, he goes down to the first floor to eat. Two children saw him walking around the house in the dark of the night several times and told their parents, but they could not believe it and thought they were nightmares.

The story doesn't end here, it is said that a few years later, this clown escaped from a mental hospital again and found the nanny girl who was the reason for his discovery and arrest, so he skinned her scalp and then cut her body into small pieces. They say and custody of the narrator that this clown is still free and takes revenge on boys and girls .. So be careful, dear reader .. I run and run away immediately if I see a clown standing in the corner of your room in the dark of the night! ...

This story and other stories, in addition to horror films, have contributed greatly to the growing fear of clowns, and there is now more than one circus where Zora is allowed to see clowns before applying powders and disguises to overcome their fear. The irony is that recent statistics have shown that a large percentage of children hate clowns because they think they are funny and ugly, and some psychologists say that few children love them.

I hope, dear / dear reader, that you enjoy my article and I am glad to hear your opinion on your view of clowns when you were children. About me When I first saw a clown in my life, I was seven years old, and I was scared of his strange look and big mouth, but then I loved them and loved the shows they do in the circus.

CITY'S LEGENDS

Most of the time, urban myths are simply (imagination) that parents might tell their kids to be careful abroad, or some friends might have wanted to spend time telling these stories on dark nights, but of course not all of these myths are a myth. Unfortunately, the weirdest and ugliest are real events.

Trade participant:

Come with me, my friend, the misfortune that fate has befallen to read this article about some of the events that abound in the story of a tortured humanity from oddities and accidents, perhaps this is not far from you, since you thought it was upsetting your mood and distorts a little the wonderful image that you may have drawn from your imagination of the world as a safe place. One can spend the happiest times of his life without being exposed to the temptation to live or die. One day it may be decided to take a vacation in the country (Moldova) This country of charming character is located in the east of the old continent, which declared its independence from the Soviet Union in 1991 and which you rarely hear about in the newsletters, and about this I formed my own opinion that a country you rarely hear about on the news is a happy country

But be careful that the wind doesn't go the way the ships would like!..

Even this peaceful state was defiled by human pests who crossed all the limits of ugliness and expanded their psychological and mental disorders in order to encroach on each other and take what was never right for them ..

We are talking about the theft of human organs! I can almost assure you that there is no one among us who has not heard the stories of people who were kidnapped and attacked until they passed out so that they could wake up later (snow bath) with a fresh and lost kidney scar. There are documented cases of similar incidents that have occurred in certain parts of the world, but especially in the countries of Moldova .. You might think that your first day at work is physically and nervously tense, but at least you are not Muhammad Salim, an Indian worker who agreed to work in a construction site near New Delhi for one extra dollar on his daily wage to get violently drugged and wake up and lost his right kidney !.

Check the bottom of the bed

Perhaps now you started to insult by wasting time reading this incident, saying, "What do I have money for Moldova and India ??! And is this portion of geography and history useless? I am the same person as a fish, if he comes out of the environment, he will die, and I would never think of leaving my homeland ... But wait, you understand that you are safe in your country? Let's take a famous story that was previously touched on at the site of a nightmare about a couple who rented a hotel room to find the unbearable smell of mold, and after extensive research, they found a rotting corpse under the mattress .. This story has already happened in many US states and took place in Las Vegas, Kansas City, Atlantic City and California. In all such cases, guests found a body under the bed, sandwiched between the mattress and the springs of the box below.

You are not alone

Well I get it !! You feel comfortable in your home and feel warm and safe, and you have no desire to leave it and book in any hotel under any circumstances. I understand how you feel and your situation ... But let me ask you a question! Do you understand that you are safe in your home? .. And what do you understand that you live alone? ? .. Let me tell you a story. There was a person who lived in his house alone - or so he thought - but every night when he came home from work, he found things inappropriate and found the food incomplete, and so the person decided to install surveillance cameras at home and when he returned from work the next day. He then showed the recorded clip during his absence to find that the cabinet was open from the inside, from which a woman was crawling into the street .. Unfortunately, he watched the clip in front of this cabinet !! ...

The man immediately ran out of the house and went to the police, who, in turn, discovered that in fact, a woman lives in this closet, who has been living for over a year !! This story is true and took place in Japan in Fukuoka, and the woman is called (Tatsuko Horikawa) At the age of 58, when investigating her, she said that she had nowhere to live and that she lived in that closet located in a room rarely used by the owner a year ago where she entered the house after the king left without closing the door! ...

Man with a strange bag

Have you ever heard of that woman who was on the bus and next to her sat a strange man in a strange bag, when she came home and watched TV, her eyes fell on the news that the patient escaped from a mental hospital and is known for his passion for removing and separating body ends? You can imagine what happened next .. In fact, psychopaths are running from every discernment and other, but that does not mean that those outside the walls of these psychiatric clinics are sane !! In 2011, at the Athens airport, a monk tried to take a suitcase full of human bones with him !! The police later discovered that these bones belonged to a nun who had died 4 years ago, and the monk claimed that he intended to return them to the monastery.

It's time to wake up

It could be from those who have a frightening vision of themselves while in an underground casing, but to find themselves still alive .. Believe it or not, but it actually happened in September 2014 for a Greek woman who was desperately trying to dig a way for outside the shroud where she was buried. Doctors believe that she tried - at least - an hour to dig her way out, but to no avail, and her family left the cemetery at that time, but fortunately, he heard her calls and cried near the graves, as well as after children who were playing.

Man-eating ladder:

Most of us - if not all of us - warned our mothers when we were young to tie our shoes long before we used the escalator, and they always warned us about it (the elevator is eating us). Obviously, we came to the conclusion that before us there were people who were exposed to this because of the strap of their continuous shoes. And again, most of us, if not all of us, beat these warnings and stories to justify the wall: the legends of the first two .. But incidents of this kind have already happened, and the reason is that the shoe strap or harness .. so on. In 2003, a little girl lost parts of her toes when she tried to get rid of shoes stuck in an escalator .. and it seems that we should pay attention not only to our laces, but to any laces in our clothes !! In another bizarre case, a hooded sweatshirt hung a shirt that a man was wearing on an escalator and a machine strangled him to death !!! ...

THE LEGEND OF LADY DEATHWHISPER

Once upon a time there was a charming beauty named Lisa, as soon as all men looked at her until they fell in love with her because of her beauty, her blonde hair fell softly on her shoulders, her eyes are blue in the color of the sky shining like the moon, her skin shines brightly from her skin, walking with vanity and bragging…

She once loved one of the men and he loved her so much and their relationship began, they met in a small hut far away because Lisa was married, her husband was very rich and loved her so much when she applied for a hand from her family, she was out of order, but had to save her family because they were severe poverty, agreed against her will and cried instead of tears .. But it makes sense for a lady of this beauty not to live a love story ???.

She always argued about going to her family's house or her friend's to meet her lover, but the days went by and her husband began to feel suspicious the day she told him she was going to her house. family, so he decided to follow her to see if she was honest or not and to doubt with certainty.

And here was the shock, he knew she was lying and followed her until she reached this hut, holding on to her nerves and waiting an hour until she came out, so he ran with all his might, he came to the house to precede her, he got home, hid a sharp knife behind his back and decided to kill her.

When she came back and found him at home, and usually at that time he was at work, I was surprised, but tried to hide it, she greeted him with a smile and asked why he was at home, so he could not stand it anymore and cried, so I went up to him and asked what was in it, so he took out a knife and put it around her neck. He cut her neck, telling her, "Why .. Why .. Why .. You did this? ?? .. how much i love you .. what a loss. ".

He killed her and then left until all her blood was bleeding and then cut her into five pieces, took her with a bag and put each piece in the place in that little hut where her lover met, and also killed her lover, seeing her severed body, cut it and laid it next to him, and then he went to his home and cut the arteries of his hand with the same knife that killed him with this.

They say that the ghost of Lisa appears in the market to seduce men with her beauty, and when she manages to seduce a man, she takes him to a distant place and then whispers in his ear: "I love you, go with me to hell." As soon as he hears these words, he becomes paralyzed, whereupon her long nails are inserted into his neck, his head is separated from his body, and his soul takes a prisoner for her, leaving him dead with blood.

Of course, most people who read this story can say that this is just a fantasy ..

But what do you think that every year the police find a person killed in such a terrible way, and the killer is unknown ?? ? .. More surprisingly, the date these bodies were found each year coincides with the same day that Lisa was killed by her husband ..

What do you think, dear readers? ... .. I leave you free to believe or deny.

DWARF FAIRIES, JIN, GILLAN OR WHAT?

Short people live very violently in the forest

As a child and whenever summer comes, we went on vacation to Tizi Ouzou state, Algeria, especially a village from the Ain el Hamam area, you can find her later to help me answer my questions..

My time was mostly boring and my grandmother, God have mercy on her, noticed that she was telling me strange stories. Perhaps that is why I love Fantasy .. My grandmother, may God have mercy on her, told me about strange creatures living in the forest, which I will describe to you..

These are short-lived people who live in the forest very fiercely and hostilely, from half a meter or less in length they are called (Tsarl) or the like. The name of Amazigh means a fairy .. The females mentioned me and did not mention the males and said that one of them had coarse hair who are so rough they don't line up, but stand in the air like Christmas trees, they have red eyes, they wear worn-out bats, their legs are wide and dirty, and their hands take a very long time to reach the ground.

In fact, the laughing stock exploded, and I told her that I was 14 years old - then - but she could not deceive me with childhood stories..

I remember very well how firmly she never joked .. I remember that she prevented me from going out at night to visit my aunt, who is her neighbor at the same time, and a few minutes before Morocco closed the doors and windows, turned off all the lights and sat down in front of the window, guarding her garden and not sleeping until she calmed us. Knowing that she does not lie and strives to fulfill the prayer ..

One day my little sister watched an animation that can then be tested as adventurers in the forest .. My grandmother came and told me that if they really don't exist, why would they show them? I told her: (My family and I only believe in the Koran and science) If they were real, where are they now, why don't you sleep in front of us and guard the garden? ,, She replied that when French colonialism came, he took dogs with him to encourage the villagers to get them to get information about the revolutionaries, these creatures fled to the mountains because they are afraid of the sound of bullets and are afraid of the bark of dogs, and that they did not guard before, but she saw that one of them was looking for food in the garbage, which means they are returning at night. So I asked her to tell me more about their stories if you like, and I will tell her one day, but the most important information about them is that they are leaving civilized areas. They love isolated villages and empty spaces. They are rebels who love to create problems. They love human flesh and sheep meat and can smell one drop of blood to determine its source, They can form and hide, They speak any language to you and love to steal and raid the property of others and fear dogs, weapons, fire, Koran and ears, especially the verse of the chair.

Dear reader, if you do decide to wander these areas one day, be sure to bring one of the five weapons we mentioned above, as they exchange and trade with you, but their violent nature tends to deceive and concoct any arguments for your accusation..

It all seems legendary, a fantasy that didn't bother me ... Of course, I love fiction and found a lot of similarities between Greek mythology and our popular stories, I told myself that this is ok due to Greece's proximity to Algeria, But what about me puzzled, so this is the coincidence of the Germanic and Scandinavian myths with the Amazigh. How can it be? And the geographic dimension known, I found that my grandmother's gnomes were like Danish trolls, I said that the mixing of civilizations in the past has led to a mixing of cultures.

I wondered why the ancients are so afraid of these creatures, despite the military development I knew at the time, and I mean rum specifically, and it is known that the imagination has an aspect of reality, which I will give you as an example ..

There is a myth about the giant squid that no one believed that this object existed and hijacked ships until it was found in Spanish waters ..

Just like the story of Hansel and Gretel, the character of the evil witch in the story is taken from people who actually ate children in hunger .. They lured them into the forest and, possibly, tricked them with a piece of candy or food.

I tried to remove the idea from my head and leave it just a legend, but his speech, may God bless him and convey balance ..

(1) Yazid bin Harun told us about Hisham bin Hasan about Al-Hasan in Jaber bin Abdullah. He said: Messenger of God, may God bless him and give him peace, said: if the ogres turn to you, call

the call to prayer.

2) Ibn Fadil told us about Al-Shaybani about Bashir bin Amr, who said: "I mentioned the ogres with his uncle, may God have mercy on him, and he said: there is nothing that could change God's creation of his creation, but they have there are magicians like yours, so if you see any of this, then please.

3) Muhammad bin Abdullah Al-Asadi told us about the son of Abi Laila about his brother Issa bin Abdul Rahman about Abdul Rahman bin Abi Laila about Abi Ayub that he was in his absence, so Gul walked, so he complained to the Prophet, may God bless him and give him peace, and he said: if you see her, say: in the name of God, answer the Messenger of God, may God bless him and give him peace, and said: he came to her, took her and said to him: I am not will be back, so he sent it, so the Prophet, may God bless him and give him peace, said to him: what did your captive do ?? He said: I took it and said: I will not return, so I sent this, and he said: he is coming back, so he took it two or three times, all this says: I am not returning, and he comes to the Prophet, may God bless him and give him peace, and he says: What did your captive do? He says: I took it and said: I will not return, so he says: she is returning; So I took it and said, "Send me and let me know that you don't say anything, Chair verse, so the Prophet, may God bless him and give him peace, came and told him, and he said: she is true and a lie. . This is a fabulous dwarves, or Jean Gillan, or what ?? .. I swear to you, your most precious thing, do not let me leave this world without knowing who they are ..

You can ask the elders and old tribes who personally met these gnomes in person, I did not see them, and my mother and aunt did not see them either, What I know is that elderly people are very peaceful and kind people who do not lied to me once, according to what I know, and all their stories about these tarmels are similar, although most of those who interrogated them and other villages do not do this to know each other.

I want to achieve that our world is full of wonders and puzzles that have not yet been discovered. I want to take advantage of our culture and study it in previous stories. They are not ignorant or stupid, as some think it is true that our ancestors did not consider technology, but I am sure they are much smarter than us, because we. We found all the requirements to live in the present and they are tired of making them live. in Khan. The least we can do is honor them by preserving their culture, which is our heritage, and the mistake of those who think that everything that the West has discovered can still do a lot and much with will, ambition and work, revealing the veil of truth

DRAGON STORY

1 - Chinese dragon:

There, in the Far East, where brightness met green straits, and far away, when the features of truth disappeared behind the curtain of imagination, the dragon was a slogan and a faith and still remains. In general, the dragon in Chinese heritage, or "Lung," as they call it, has a symbol of goodness and virtue as it expresses beauty and strength. As for his apparent form, this follows from the symbolism he acquired in the Chinese heritage, as he is characterized by the strength of structure and visual acuity, he has four lists and a body similar to the bodies of snakes in his flexibility and expansion, in addition to his ability shoot from the mouth that is covered with fangs, it can fly or swim in deep water. Oceans and humid places represent the ideal environment for this creature to live and the stage in which most of its stories revolve with humans.

Historically, the fact that the dragon has long been a symbol of goodness and strength in the Chinese faith has given it ample place in the art world of all kinds. And the dragon was a symbol of imperial China and its creation until 1912, when the republic was founded by Sun Yat Sen. It is worth noting that the dragon has been the emblem of many kingdoms and alliances in various parts of East Asia, and a country like Bhutan still adopts it as a state emblem. In life, the dragon has become a reality in society that the Chinese people live through their statues in ancient temples or archaeological palaces. In the past, Chinese silk dresses were adorned with paintings, and his inscriptions on these dresses have become an approved brand for them. And show a drawing of Leon Al-Kiliki, an Armenian, wears one of these dresses.

Far from tangible art and heritage, the Chinese people hold the dragon with gratitude and respect in all areas of their lives. Just as they view the month of the dragon (one of the months of the Chinese year) as a month of development and prosperity, they believe that every child in it will enjoy health and well-being in their lives. And in the expressions of modern Chinese, the dragon is considered a title for those who have power and influence, especially if we know the extent of their belief in its ability to rain and move various components of nature, such as water and wind, and these beliefs gave it a piece of divinity. and holiness among the people of China.

2- European dragon:

Among the folds of ancient books was the story of the European dragon, which tells the epithelyms of the sacrifice and the fathers. Inspired by the heritage of the ancients, the legend with the most pleasant stories went to the pens of writers. To start telling the story of the European dragon, we must touch on its origins and the peculiarities of its origin through its name and its roots. Linguistically, most European designations called dragon, such as English "dragon" and German "fighter," return their origin to the Latin word "draco", which in turn means caution, caution, or careful observation. It is noted here that "Draco" refers to the Greek word for "Dragon", it is a canvas doll in the shape of a dog or a wolf used by ancestral people in the past in their wars in a manner similar to the flag as indicated in the inscriptions of the Trajan Archaeological Column in Rome, and these inscriptions depict one of the campaigns of the Roman emperor Trajan over the Kingdom of Dacia, southeastern Europe. Like the Chinese dragon, it has a crust of skin and an excellent ability to shoot from its hollow. The European dragon has two large wings, like the wings of a bat, and a solid tail that can defend itself. And through repeated reading in the heritage we find many of his characteristics, and among the most prominent of these characteristics were the magical benefits of his blood that make his mustache able to understand the language of a bird. European peoples have always viewed the dragon as a hostile and evil entity, and this point of view was established in the Middle Ages by tales, which he always depicts as the guardian of treasures kept in castles or caves. Although we find that myths in Eastern Europe often refer to dragons as twins, the man is the protector of the people, unlike his twin woman, which symbolizes unrest and harm. And contrary to the image conveyed by these tales and heritage, the dragon has become the slogan for one of the provinces and cities in various parts of Europe, such as the British province of Wales and the city of Ljubljana, the capital of Slovenia. And this position that the dragon has acquired can be traced back to his portrayal as the protector of wealth and the owner of hostile traits against the aggressors against him, who created an indirect form of father or patriotism. And this opinion can support me from what was in the war of two civil roses. As part of this war, which took place over three decades, the York family made the Red Dragon a symbol during the Battle of Bo Sort, while the white pig was the emblem of the Lancaster family. When I started my conversation about the European dragon, I ended it with a relationship between a man and a legend. An amazing change and a coup d'état. And with the wave of cartoons like the Shrek movie series, the root of that change has been, and the pillars of that coup have been fixed. From a cruel creature to a pet and from an object that expresses evil, the symbol of nationalism and fatherhood has emerged.

THE WORLD OF MYTHS (MONSTERS).

There is nothing in this material world that can attract and attract the minds of people. This is the real world, which has only its own surprises and paranormal phenomena. Therefore, since ancient times, people have resorted to legends to waste their time and entertainment, and sometimes to be afraid of the young. Myths spread throughout the world until every nation had a myth, and the myths differed from place to place. Children and adults used to listen to him. but some believe in it and believe in the existence of mythical creatures .. Is it really present, or is the legend still a myth that has no right to penetrate the fence of reality?!..

Legend 1 .. Ohio giant frog ..

The story began in 1972 when a police officer reported that he saw him as a giant sticky monster that looked like a 2.1m frog and walked with two legs, and he saw him on the side of the road when he was driving a car at night in the US state of Ohio. and another officer followed, observing the scary giant frog .. Then rumors began to spread .. (In Ohio and other American states, there is a type of frog known as the pale cricket frog that makes a sound like marble pieces clashing together ..

Why is this fictional? ..

The local police investigated to find any evidence to support the existence of this creature, but they did not find anything, and moreover, one of the officers later admitted that people greatly exaggerated his story and that he believed that what he saw , maybe a kind of (War) Alif, who grew up in houses and some types are three meters long - and he went out and lost his way ..

Legend 2 .. Disgusting ice man ..

The monster's hair floats around the peaks of Asia. Perhaps a legend (Yeti) originated. The hideous ice man in Tibet, a region close to the Himalayan mountain range in Asia, is said to have ugly creatures with thick hair that look like a hybrid of a man and a bear and have frightening fangs. The story of this monster has been published by a nomad known as a Sherpa since the sixteenth century when he roamed Nepal. And around him, the story is still in Tibet, and some claim to see this monster.

Why is this a fictional story?

In 2013, a scientist examined the DNA of hair strands that were said to belong to ((IT)) _ the disgusting ice man _ and were taken from where he should have been. The results showed that the hair did not come from an unknown monster, but it is the type of old polar bear that may live in the region, and it is likely that those who claimed to have seen the ice man only saw this bear.

Legend 3 .. (Dobarsho) ..

Or a water dog, half of which is a domestic fox (Ireland) .. No one knows exactly where the legend about this beast came from, but the legend began to appear at least in the eighteenth century after the appearance of a sculpted statue of the beast on the grave of one of the alleged victims. It is assumed that these creatures live in the lakes of Ireland and emit a sound signal. She has an appetite for people's food.

Why is this a fictional story? ..

Basically this monster is a Eurasian otter, where these animals were found in rivers and lakes in Ireland and it is likely that this horn is their way of communicating

Legend 4 .. Chuba Kabra Monster ..

(((Blood of farm animals))) .. In the nineties of the twentieth century, many goats and chickens died in many areas b (Puerto Rico) Strange, her blood was bleeding and gradually drying up and the legend of the monster began (Chupacabra) Rumor had it, that he is a criminal and that he is a monster, like a vampire, with a frightening form, with fangs and a forked tongue, with sharp spines on his back, and later a wave of such deaths appeared a few years later in his state (Tskas) He accused the monster (Chupacabra) Who translates to (Goat Vampire) In Spanish ..

Coyotes are often seen as a deceiving animal in the Native American (Native American) folk heritage of the state (Tescas) and other states in the southwestern United States.

Why is this a fictional story?

The death of the chickens was confirmed and there was no evidence that her blood was drained. It is possible that what they consider to be Chub Kabra's monster mother is sick coyotes or a dog. Try: because deformation of the skin can show the animal in a frightening way ..

Legend 5 .. (Kongamato) ..

It is a monster of flying reptiles attacking boat passengers in Africa. The origin of the story is unknown, but the word Konhamato means in African language (Boat crusher) They are said to be huge monsters that flew low over the swamps of South and Central Africa and have skin wings and a mouth full of sharp teeth and it is rumored that they are jumping from sky to destroy and crush boats, and this myth dates back almost a long time ..

Why is this a fictional story?

Scientists see an animal (Congamato) It is not a winged reptile that became extinct more than 65 million years ago, and what is believed to be the Kunga Mato monster may be a giant hammer bat that lives in swamps and is one of the largest bats (Africa) Where its wing stretches 90 centimeters in length, or it could be a huge demon fish and it was seen jumping into boats ..

THE STORY OF LA EURONA .. LEGEND OR FACT?

La Loroona, or the weeping woman, is a story that has been spread across generations and told children to scare them.

The story of a crying woman is a sad story, and at the same time terrifying, many people say that the story is true .. What do you see, who is not Euroona? ?? What's her story? ??

Many years ago, a girl named Maria lived in a small village and was very beautiful, and all the villagers loved her for her tenderness and beauty ..

She said herself that she was the most beautiful girl in the world, and she did not care about the youth of the village, she always said: I will marry the most beautiful man in the world .. !!

One day, a young man named Ranchero appeared with the same characteristics as Faris Dream Maria, who was the son of a wealthy herder, was handsome and had a beautiful voice. He charmed everyone around him when he played the harp and sang his sweet voice.

Maria loved him very much and thought that the young man loved her too and she wanted to win and she wanted to get his attention more and Ranchero wanted to talk to Maria, but she claimed she didn't give a damn about him to get his attention more.

Every day Ranchero came to the door of Maria's house, played and sang to show Maria, but although she could hear and sing for his singing, she pretended to be indifferent ..

Keel Ranchero was amazed to win Maria .. He told her that he loved him, so they got married and had two children ..

At first, everything was fine for two, but days and years passed, and one day Ranchero decided to travel and missed a few months, and upon returning home Maria noticed that he had changed, he was only interested in seeing his children, and did not show interest in his wife Maria.

A few months later, Ranchiro left home and married a young girl younger than Maria Sen.

One day Maria and her two sons were walking to a place by the river, and she found Ranchero and his new young wife, riding in a carriage. When Ranchero saw his children, he got out of the cart and started hugging them, not paying attention to Maria, as if she was not there, so Maria got angry and angry .. She wanted to take revenge on her husband and burn his heart when she burned her heart, so she got pregnant and transferred the tumor to the river .. After I calmed down a bit, I found out how wrong it was, I regretted it, jumped to the river and started looking for two boys who were washed away by the stream of water ..

I took to watch and watch ... But to no avail .. She never found her two sons until she was tired ..

The next morning one of the men passed this river, and he found a very beautiful woman, dead on the river bank .. Mary is dead looking for her children, who killed her by hand.

From that day, the legend of La Eurona began ...

The villagers said they saw a beautiful woman in white clothes who was waving, "My children? !! Where are you, my children? ? !!

That's why they called it "La Eurona" .. That is, a crying woman.

Legend has it that this is a punishment for Mary because her soul could not ascend to heaven until she brought her children, so she spins and revolves all over the earth in search of her children. It is said that sometimes when she finds children near their homes at night, she takes them and drowns them in the river in the hope that she will be allowed to ascend to heaven with their souls instead of her children. But her trick is always revealed and she is sent back to earth to roam into it until the day they are resurrected.

People in Mexico believe that they do not see us coming out of rivers and lakes in the evening and wander as they cry in search of their children, and it is said that hearing her voice cry is a bad omen, and that soon after that everyone who dies. hears the sound of her crying at night.

Some say that this story is a figment of the imagination of the mother and grandmother .. She tells her children about the desire to scare them and not let them go out at night. Others say that the story is real, and it really happened ...

Dear readers, you can believe or deny the story.

SELFISH GIANT - FROM ENGLISH HERITAGE -

Wherever he danced and moved this boy, winter under his feet turned to spring!

Once upon a time .. In a village in the English countryside there was a beautiful garden called (Giant Park) ..

The giant garden owner has just returned from a long journey and it is strange that the giant initially forgot the reason for leaving his garden! .. Since he immigrated her a long time ago, and then he was eighteen years old, that is, 30 years ago, yes .. The fastest years have passed, thirty years have passed since he left his beautiful garden, and he did not know about the changes that took place in this place during these continuous years.

Upon arrival, he was surprised by a group of young people playing, shivering and having fun in his beautiful garden, so he got very angry, drove them all out and built a high fence around the garden so that the children would not be allowed to pass again.

The giant was left alone in his garden .. He thinks for a long time about the reason why he left the park and went on a long journey .. He continued to think and think until winter .. But he never remembered and did not realize the reason! ..

The winter has been really long, and of course spring should start after it, but this time it seems that winter has been going on for so long that the giant starts to get upset.

What a strange phenomenon! Spring has come to the whole valley for a long time, but spring has not come to the giant garden! Surrounded by a high fence .. Because of a storm, there was a break in the garden fence, so the children entered from under it, and suddenly winter turned into a spring! ..

By the spring, the giant was very scared, but he soon became upset when he found the children playing in the garden, so he kicked them all out, so winter was back again and the cruel giant was surprised! ..

Suddenly he found a standing boy who didn't go and he collapsed saying: Hey boy why didn't you go with the kids? .. Let's get out of here!

So, the boy began to jump and dance, and the ground under his feet turned from a cold earth without life into trees, flowers and basil .. Thus, winter turned into a warm spring again ..

The giant realized that a place where children cannot enter never starts in spring .. Then he baptized the wall of his beautiful garden and destroyed it .. Children were allowed to enter, and since spring he never left the park ..

Years and years passed and age progressed like a giant, but he was happy that he was always surrounded by gay children ..

One day the giant was sitting looking at the children playing and having fun in his garden, so he muttered to himself, saying:

- How much I miss seeing that wonderful child who danced around the winter of my heart in the spring .. Unfortunately, this is not a second for us .. What do you see now? ,,

She gave up other long years, and the age of the giant has advanced significantly, and now he is preparing for a sleepless journey ...

Suddenly this child appeared again .. And the giant said in ink, although he was dying on his bed

- Oh .. You are my dear !! ..

With his wonderful smile, the child said:

- I came to take you ..

And the giant said:

- Welcome, dear .. Of course, I am ready to go with you, I thank you, thanks to you I knew the meaning of spring and the taste of warmth .. Thank you from the depths .. From the depths, my dear ..

The child added, saying:

Do you remember why I left the park many years ago?

The giant replied:

- Yes .. Yes, I remembered .. I was alone and I lived in a cruel and painful unit, I am very sorry for the loss of this precious time of my life, my dear .. Yes, believe me ..

And the child said:

- I really realized that over time, but you are not the only one who suffers from loneliness, there are many people like you in this world for various reasons ... Let's go on a long journey now, but this time you will not be alone, I will be with you ..

The giant and the boy went to the afterlife, where absolute happiness, lasting comfort, acquaintance and endless eternal warmth in the arms of mercy ..

With this our story ended .. I hope to find a wonderful lesson in this and not close doors on two roads, regardless of their nature, we do not appreciate the value of things, except when they are lost .. Hold on to your loved ones ..

TWO STARS .. A TALE OF CHINESE HERITAGE

These two stars are Flying Eagle and Reality Eagle, they only meet once a year .. So why is this happening ?? This story will explain to you why ..

Once upon a time there lived a very poor man named (Alkir) In a remote area, He took full care of his old bull, After they did the hard work, Cyrus dried the sweat on his forehead, rested, and began playing the flute for his revolution. and landed playing a dove next to him, He told her, Do you like to play with me, dove? .. The dove turned into a girl, and the young man was surprised and said to her: who are you ??

And she told him: my name is (Vika), I live in the highest mountains, and I liked that you play the flute, so I came to listen, and he really told her that you are a good girl, Vika .. Thank you for your compliment ..

He asked her to dance to his beautiful tones, so she danced to Vika while she was happy with the beautiful flute tones, and she could fly, so she flew as a dancer into the sky while the kir played amazed ..

After the game was over, Vika asked Cyrus to leave, He begged her to stay because he wanted to marry her, She refused and told him that their laws did not allow this, He kept asking her until she agreed after hesitating, Vika married Alkir and forgot the laws of her family, which do not allow her to marry a man, except for her family or city ..

One day, Vicki's father went to the couple's house while they were sleeping, so he woke up his daughter and took her with him on a cloud and rosy, Al-Kir noticed that Vika had lost a lot of sadness, so he told him: come on, straight to them quickly , you still have time

Al-Kir said, surprised: yes, you speak like people?

And his revolution told him: yes .. But come on quickly and catch them.

He said to him: how?

The bull asked him to wear Vicky's feather cloak because it would allow him to fly. But when the kir followed them and asked his father to take Vika, his father did not allow him to do this, Al-Kir begged him, but all his requests were in vain, the Father thought of an idea that would make Al-Keir change his idea of continuing to marry Vika. He was offered a box of jewelry in exchange for forgetting Vika and leaving immediately, but Al-Qir rejected the offer and he said that there was no comparison between the jewelry box and Vika, so the father could not separate them and he was very angry, throwing the ball into a valley full of predatory monsters eager to kill, but it seemed that Al-Kir insisted on his command, clinging to Vika, and defeated the monsters, and returned to join his wife and father ..

He fell into the hands of Vicki's father, but he thought and found a way to be incapable of disaster, so he asked him to suppress his strange revolution, claiming that it prolongs life, and told him: kill your bull and take my daughter, .. Al-Qair could not kill my revolution ..

The father separated Al-Kira and Vika, placing a river between them, Vika rebelled against her father and threatened him to drown in the river if she was not allowed to go with the kir, so her father suggested that she meet with the kir once a year, She agreed to his proposal , It's better for her than her death, so I don't see him again ..

Since then, the couple met once a year, and this meeting is called by the Chinese (Tana_Bata) ..

Thus, the story ended.

Don't forget to look up to the sky and continue with Tana Bata ..

THE LEGEND OF MERLIN AND EXCALIBUR'S SWORD

England is a beautiful magical country located on an archipelago that includes four countries: England, Ireland, Scotland and Wales. These are all known (with the exception of the Republic of Ireland) as Great Britain or Great Britain. Of course, I will not dwell on the description of England, since it is self-evident. Who among us has not heard about the city of fog London or King Henry VIII and the story of his crazy love for Anne Boleyn and his murders of his wives or a series of films about Harry Potter and the master of seals or the great writer William Shakespeare ..

And since the English heritage is replete with stories and myths that are said to be the least wonderful, I have chosen for you, my dear readers, two legends in such a way that they relate to each other .. Please enjoy your reading.

Merlin the white magician

In Middle Abal and the masters of hell planned to bring the absolute prince of darkness to compete and destroy Christ, the Demon manipulated a virgin village girl and made her pregnant, but soon she realized her mistake and realized that she had become a victim of blind love and did not know the essence of her devilish lover and his dirty scheme, so she vowed that the rest of her life would live in pure service to the Lord, She was pregnant with Merlin (Merlin) And I drank holy waters, and as a result this boy was born with supernatural powers, but with good intentions and did not seek destroy people, but vice versa, to save them.

Merlin's childhood

The British king Fortigen tried to defend his kingdom from the Saxons (German tribes invade) He built a tower in the Snowia mountains, But the priests told him that it was impossible to defeat the enemies unless blood was spilled for the fatherless children, This component was difficult to obtain, Where they would take the child without a father? ,, Dear reader, we are talking about medieval Europe, where the concept of purity, adultery and chastity was completely different from what exists in the West today, That is why it was difficult to find a child without a father, But the priests searched and searched until they found their wrong leadership in Merlin, And who soon discovered what the Druidic sorcerers were planning, These were the priests and wizards of England in ancient times before Christianity, Away from the world of myths, the Druidic priests were truly terrible, They have frightening and gruesome rituals of human sacrifice that include the burning of sacrifices alive, Returning to the story of Merlin, the plan of the magicians was originally to destroy Merlin, Through magic and astrology, they knew that he would become a great magician, compete with them and win the king's favor, They wanted to kill him, But Merlin survived the murder with his mind and extraordinary abilities He told the king that the magicians had missed an important thing, That if the tower is built, it is not will last for the deep pond below him, in which the cave fights with two dragons, one red and the other white, Merlin, with his extraordinary abilities, could see this, The King changed his murder.

Merlin and King Arthur

The Welsh legend of King Arthur was occupied by (King Arthur) A prominent place in British mythology and world literature.Many films have been filmed around Merlin and Excalibur.There are those who considered him a leader who actually existed and there are those who considered him half god my basket and half human, But its existence is lost or not a mystery that has inspired many English writers in both old and modern times.

Arthur Pendragon, according to ancient myths, is a brave king, a dragon hunter, a veteran fighter and a hero in every sense of the word, combining nobility and generosity and protecting the poor and the oppressed. He grew up in Gwyneth, North Wales and loved one woman, and most loyal to her was Guenever, who became his queen after he crowned king over Camelot, the name of the kingdom of Arthur, which he founded from the remains of his ruined village by the Saxons. Arthur and his wife Guinniver have a famous story, as her heart clung to the love of one of Arthur's friends from the Knights of the Round Table, Knight Lancelot, and this forbidden love ended in tragedy and caused Arthur's death, and it is a long story to which we can return for one day .

The magician Merlin predicted the birth of Arthur and that he would take Excalibur and lead the battle between good and evil and defeat him. Merlin later became Arthur's right-hand advisor and an important member of the roundtable for the protection of the Holy Grail, which was a symbol of Christian connotations, but with depth and respect, dating back to the days of Paganism. This table was a symbol of Arthur and his brave knights.He had a prominent position in the Church Arthur's end is unclear. There are those who say that he died in the Battle of Kamlan in 537 AD by the spy of Mordraut, who was sent by the druid magicians and is said to have survived and was taken to the island of Avalon, and he was treated and will one day, return when his people desperately need it, They believe it strongly, especially the people of Wales, Cronol and Brittany, Until King Henry VIII is said to have sought Arthur's grave to exhume his body and his alleged grave under the rock that is what they claim is the rock of Excalibur, But the grave was found empty. There are myths that Arthur sleeps deep in a cave and wakes up one day. The bottom line is that King Arthur has taken a large place in the English heritage, and the British may not have another king at all.

Merlin's End

There are several novels about the end of the white magician. Some believe that his father's demons took him to hell, It is also said that he mysteriously disappeared, But the most famous of all is that he fell in love with his student, Nevin, who was the lady of the lake She used this to teach her magic, and she would become strong and immortal like him, And when he surpassed him, he locked him in a castle, cave, or grave, and the prisoner lost his love, suffering, and remorse forever, Though he was the strongest and most experienced of magicians, turning his beloved against him and his betrayal with him or his discovery that she did not love him at all, rather a means of achieving interests that made him weak and destroyed forever.

Whatever the fate of Merlin, his fame has never been fulfilled and he is perhaps the most famous magician in the world, as he has mentioned in many stories and novels, and his personality has been embodied in many films, TV series and plays. Perhaps the closest to him from memory is the 2008 Merlin series, which was very popular and very successful and is a product of the BBC

The Legend of Excalibur

It is a myth that speaks of a legendary sword that sits in a large stone, waiting for a strong hand to wrap around his neck like a touch or a caring mother, arrest him by the power of a lion and wrap around him like a snake, then he entertained him from the rocky shell to touch the rays of light and the breath of the wind

In many Scandinavian countries and the United States of America, festivals associated with the Middle Ages are sometimes held.The most important characteristic of these festivals is the presence of a stone with a false sword, of course, and whoever retrieves it is rewarded with a stuffed cotton bear or any other gift. But this game didn't come out of nowhere, it has deep legendary roots to know.

Excalabur / Caliburn is a sword with magical powers from the property of King Arthur, created by Merlin to protect Camelot a thousand years before Arthur was born.Arthur is said to have taken him from the cliff in the midst of a bloody battle, illuminating his magical light and causing blindness on all his enemies , so he defeated the forces of evil .. Legend has it that the one who holds the sword never bleeds and never dies in battle. This sword is also a symbol of people's honor, and it is said that one of the nobles demanded from those who propose to offer his daughter to remove the heavy iron sword from the stone! ...

There is a local legend that in the past, the village blacksmiths were united to make the largest and heaviest sword, and then empty the cement and leave it dry.One day, people meet and become a festival of male muscle power, Anyone who manages to remove the sword , is a hero and welcomes him, As for the loser, the sword will inflict his whole life, or until he leaves the village.

Another famous story is the story of the daughter of the Marquis, who loved the groom, Of course, her father would never agree to marry his daughter to a poor, disadvantaged young man, He, Any Marquis, He does not believe in the language of love, as in the language of money and social classes, He accidentally gave his daughter a clumsy young man, but he is the son of a wealthy merchant, According to the oppressive father, this clumsy was a suitable husband for his daughter, He has money, But the daughter refused and accused her father of injustice and injustice, The father wanted to make a play in which he appeared as a just father, he organized a competition that required the groom and the rich son to try to remove the sword from the rock, and whoever succeeds in this will receive the hand of the marquis's daughter.

People gathered to see the competition, This day was a great holiday and celebration, But what people don't know is that the marquis deliberately cheated in the competition so that Ibn Al-Tura would win, He ordered the blacksmiths to make the heaviest sword and put it down into double layers of cement and hard-to-break materials for the stables.As for the merchant's son, he ordered them to make a sword that scared metal, easy to carry, and put it in a rock with a large hole to ensure his victory.

The stable was a huge corpse, Everyone is betting on his victory, On the other hand, it was clear that the spoiled son of Al-Tri did not work even once in his life and shivered like a chicken and walked in hesitation, pamper himself like girls, Although the marquis only made his mission easier, he could not take off his sword every time and rested from every attempt to the next, As for the stable, he never stopped trying, His mission was almost impossible, Everyone thought it would fail, But while he was resting from repeated attempts, he looked at his beloved and saw tears in the eyes of the witches, so he screamed loudly, grabbed the sword, and pulled it with all the force that came until his hands were bleeding, These are just moments until the sword is removed from its place among the cries, the encouragement and amazement of the masses.

But despite the groom's heroism, the father of his beloved refused to marry his daughter on the pretext that the sword he had removed remained part of him, broken in the rock.And when people noticed the marquis's injustice, they encouraged his daughter to flee with her lover and blocked way from her father and his followers, until the two lovers fled to an unknown place to live happily.

It is worth noting that the legendary sword was not always perceived as a legend.There are those who believed that it was a real sword and that it was very large and heavy, given that the ancient warriors were a huge corpse, And that the sword was made of gold mixed with platinum metal , which gives him super strength, He is dotted with blue exhalations, red sapphire and emerald coating, In his fist there is a large pearl, a moonstone ... This extravagant description of the sword prompted many archaeologists to search for it in order to preserve it as a national treasure, But At the same time, this description sparked greed in the hearts of many.Treasure hunters and gangsters gathered from all over the world, They desecrated the graves of many ancient knights in search of the tomb of King Arthur and his legendary sword, with which he was believed to have been buried. But there is another myth that, after his death, his wife, Gwinniver, melted the sword and changed it in the form of coins, which she gave to the poor.There are those who say that the sword was stolen by the French and then lost in the Atlantic Ocean in the result of the storm that destroyed the ship, And some English people today still blame the French, but we know that history is only a disguise because the reasons for the true animosity between the two parties are political and have something to do with competition and historical hatred between the majority neighboring countries and peoples.

Dear Sirs! If you have ever had the opportunity to visit the UK, feel free to stop by museums, ask them about their history and myths and watch their plays .. Indeed, this is a fictional world with a special charm and the people of the ancient island have added a unique flavor.

METHODOLOGY AMONG THE GREEKS

In ancient old age, which was pardoned for years and covered with books among its folds, myths were an integral part of their daily life, thus people find their simplicity by spreading these myths as a kind of entertainment and entertainment, or as a story they tell children before going to bed. and you can find it in those who considered these myths to be a pillar essential in his life and an idea based on his religious and worldly faith.

Greeks (Ancient Civilization of Greece) They are the source of most of those myths that we hear today, although their civilization played an important role in the development of science of all kinds, and from their crucifixion came the most famous philosophers in history, but their civilization was not without some myths. that are ingrained in their minds, something that confused me is just how civilization like the Greeks can believe in such myths. They consider people of logic, and it was they who exported this flag to the whole world. In this article I will talk about some of the myths known in the Greek civilization ..

The Legend of Narxus

To learn the legend of Narksus, we must first learn Echo, Echo is super beautiful, a nymph in a sweet tongue, always having fun on the shores of lakes and between forests, sitting on the top of a plateau overlooking the lake, watching all the passers-by calmly and serenely, one day he saw (An echo on the great deity of Zeus, who is with the nymph of beautiful showers, whispering together and happiness floods their faces, and after a while her vision fell on the goddess Hera (Zeus's Wife) I am looking for something with indignation that seemed to split her face, nymph Eko stopped Zeus's wife (Hera) And I asked her about the reason for her anger, and the latter replied that he was looking for his traitorous husband Zeus. He crept into her hearing that her husband had moved from this place with a beautiful nymph, then I asked her, whether she saw her husband and her last answer with denial, Hera decided to continue her research, but Eko invited her to sit with her and talk, and after taking and handing over, Hera agreed to sit with Eko, a conversation between them began to take place, and Hera was impressed the sweetness of San Eco and the sweetness of her conversation to such an extent that time passed quickly without feeling it, and the fires of anger began to extinguish inside Hera, I looked to Eru at the horizon and she found the sun, asking permission to set, then she saw her husband Zeus when he threw himself into the realm of the gods in heaven, so she got angry and decided to take revenge on Eko, because she covered Zeus and took revenge on the gods hard, so she punished her by holding her sweet tongue and Eko could not speak, Just the last words of the speaker were indecisive, and Echo continued to play in the lakes and forests, and his beauty grew day by day.

Narxus is a very handsome young man who admired the beauty of all those who saw him, be it from gods, humans or even nymphs, but at the same time he was arrogant and arrogant with his beautiful beauty and does not allow love to go the way to his heart. One morning Narksus went with his friends to the side (Forest for hunting, and as usual, Eko sat on the top of the plateau, quietly watching passers-by, until she saw a very handsome young man (Narksus) She loved him at first sight and wanted to go to him, but she preferred to look at him in silence, fearing that she would not be able to speak, because she knew that Nerkus never meant love,

Nerkus and his companions looked at the group of victims and rushed to chase them, the prey was separated from each other and FriendsIn in turn, each of them stalking their prey, Narksus went after his prey, chasing and spraying it with deadly arrows, trying to strike it in deadly places, and after lair and fur, Nerkus was able to hit his prey and throw it to the ground, but soon he noticed that he had moved away from his friends, faster Narksus is looking for his friends, and he does not know that there is a wandering lover with his love who runs after him wherever he goes. Narksus sat next to the lake sighing and he lost hope of finding his friends, so he called them and the nymph repeated the last words he spoke ..

The nymph did not hold on, so she rushed to Nerkus, stretching out her arms to hug him, but the latter, in turn, moved away to fall Eko on her face, Narxus threw the nymph with cold looks, as if he mocked what happened to her as the latter got up and fled, retaining the remnants of her dignity that were scattered before Narksus, Narksus returned to his friends. He rejoiced in his victory over Eko and spoke arrogantly to them about what had happened to him.

Days went by and Eko still fell in love with Nerkus and the latter becomes more beautiful day by day as he fades over the days due to the sadness buried inside him until the day Eko disappeared and became an echo reflecting his voice the speaker, the goddess of love Aphrodus did not get up. It happened to Eko. Aphrodite's job was to take revenge on the outcast lovers, so she decided to punish Nerkus for his deed with Eko.

Narxus and his friends went fishing as usual and separated two hours behind their prey. Narkus began stalking his prey until he was tired, so he sat breathing next to the roaring water, so Narkus drank DNA from betrayal to drink. He saw a human image in the water, more beautiful than the moon hanging from the sky. His eyes smiled at this beautiful face, to smile at the other in turn, he began to wave his hand at him, so the other in turn, Narxus returned to his house, and the noise of his thoughts was never merciful, because he admired what he saw and could not sleep at night , so he quickly returned to Ghadeer, and when he arrived, he walked over the head of his fingers, fearing that his sleeping lover would wake up in Ghadeer, and the moon at that time illuminated this place with silver rays, DNA from betrayal to find his lover, more does not sleep, and he was happy, because he thought that his beloved was still waiting for him, he told him, "I love you." He saw his lover moving his lips in the water with the same word, he returned to his home and the image of a man in water does not leave his imagination, and his love increases day by day.

Days passed and sadness began to weave its webs in the same Nercusus, because he thought that his lover did not want to talk to him, so his return and his beauty were ignored, then he passed away when he said :. Goodbye who loved goodbye.

Echo Echo: Oh who I love goodbye.

Of course, the beautiful face that Narksus saw in Gadera was only a reflection of his image on the surface of the water, and this punishment imposed on him by the goddess Aphrodtus, Echo's voice continued to repeat what the travelers were saying and crossed the roads, while Narksus pardoned gods and brought him back to life, but not as a man. It was only flowers that sprouted near the lakes, called "nergus flowers", and hence it was called.

The Legend of Semiramis, the daughter of the bathroom

Once, a large egg was floating on the Euphrates, and there were two large fish trying to push this egg to the beach, but a large dove landed from the sky, which hugged the egg and took it with him to the nest and remained lying on the egg until it hatched, and the girl removed the moon from his place to the seriousness of her beauty, the dove and her friends flapped their wings to the girl until he realized it from the sun's heat, and at night he hugged her to be sure of his cold, the pigeons were confused about how they would feed little girl, so they decided to look for a place inhabited by people so that they could find their misfortune there, and indeed, they fell on a sheepdog farm. They took what the shepherd made from milk and cheese, just as their beaks expanded, the shepherd noticed the pigeons' access to his farm every day and noticed that the pigeons landed in a place not far from the farm, so he and his friends decided one day to follow the pigeons and really followed them to find the beautiful lying girl, their nest, they took this girl with them to the farm and decided to sell her in the market of Nineveh especially on the wedding day.

The wedding day came, and beautiful young shepherds entered the market of Nineveh to sell it, and the day of the market was overflowing with young and old. The former wanted to find a bride to marry her, and the latter wanted to buy a girl so that his son would marry her, especially (the royal rider) On this beautiful girl who was sterile and without offspring, he decided to buy her and accept it. Indeed, it happened. Seema returned with the boy to his home and his wife was happy about it and they continued to educate her until her return intensified and her femininity was finished and she became more beautiful than her beauty.

One day, Semiramis was among a group of people, overwhelmed by the order of the king, and "Ones" caught the eye (Royal advisor) On Smiramis, he admired her beauty and decided to marry her, took her to the market of Nineveh and married her there, lived with love and harmony, and over time they had two twin children, "Hefat" and "Heidasga" The day came when King Ninos gathered his armies to invade the country of Pakteria, and he was able to do so, with the exception of the capital " Bakra ". She was able to withstand the royal army. The king got confused and decided to send "Ones" for his advisor to help him in military affairs. Nobody wanted to leave his beautiful wife, so he invited her to go with him, so the latter indicated acceptance and went together to the king and his soldiers.

They and Semiramis arrived on the battlefield, and Smiramis began to study the war in detail and make plans for the coming battles. The battle was easy then, so Smiramis asked the king to send a crowd of soldiers trained to fight in the mountains until they surrounded the capital in all respects, because the mountains surrounded it from all sides, and indeed the city was besieged in all respects, so the capital announced that obeys the command of King Ninos, at that time the king admired the most admired of Smirah and decided to take him away from his adviser in exchange for the latter giving his daughter, but the adviser refused this deal, and the king threatened to gouge out his eyes and found an adviser who forced himself to obey the orders of the king, and immediately announced his approval, and after several days of the king's marriage to Semiramis, the consultant committed suicide because he could not end his life away from his beloved.

The king had a child by Smiramis who called him "Ninas" and after a while the king passed away and she received the reigning Smiramis until her son reached the most severe and made a decision on her.

Note: Queen Smiramis is herself the Queen of Iraq "Sammuramat" and the Greeks misrepresented the queen's name and her life to make her the legend of their legends.

Jellyfish legend

The three sisters were famous for their picturesque beauty (Sthino, Earl and Medusa) They lived at the end of the world, Medusa, the daughter of the sea god "Portia", who was famous for her beauty and picturesque eyes, the day came and Medusa committed a sin with "Poseidon" (Another sea god) In the temple of Athena (Daughter of Zeus, the main deity), Athena became angry and cursed her on Medusa, turning her silky hair into poisonous snakes, and as another punishment, everyone who looks at her eyes turns into worn stones, despite to the punishment that happened on Medusa, she ignored it and practiced her life naturally.

Medusa went too far in her family, and everyone looking at her eyes turned to stones so that no one could kill her, Perseus rose (Greek hero) Preparation for battle was necessary (Sharp sword to cut off her head, Hermes shoes for flight, a bag with a head so as not to offend anyone with eyes that turn those who look at them into stones, Minerva's shield and the Hadith helmet must be hidden so that you do not see Medusa) He went to Medusa and saw her where she did not see him, then with a sudden blow, he beheaded, after Perseus killed Medusa, he hung his head on Minerva's shield, and Medusa's eyes still retain her strength, everyone who looks at her turns into stones, rewarded Perseus eternity for defeating Medusa.

Legend of Prometheus

Prometheus is the chief advisor to the gods of Zeus and was known for his ability to predict the future. One day Zeus commissioned Prometheus and his brother Avimetheus to shape humans and animals, so they both began their work. Prometheus is in charge of the formation of humans, and his brother is in charge of the formation of animals (Avimetius quickly formed animals, while his brother Prometheus wanted to make humans in the best way and as a result of his delay, Abimeteus used most of the resources available (Speed, strength, fangs, claws , visual acuity, hearing and fur, which protects them from the cold .. etc. In the education of animals, Prometheus could use little. Prometheus resorted to Zeus, perhaps giving him some traits to put in people, but Zeus was outraged people and did not want to give them anything, forcing Prometheus to steal gifts from the Olympian gods (Hephaestus, Athena and others) This gave people reason, architecture, astronomy, numbers and letters, and how they use Avimetius animals for riding.

With all the gifts Prometheus gave people, he forgot to give them fire to keep warm, so he decided to go to the headquarters of "Hephaestus" (Mourning of the Gods) Secretly so that Zeus would not know about his command, punished him and stole a lightning strike from his lightning to give it to the people, Prometheus went to Hephaestus' headquarters and slightly managed to steal one of Zeus's lightning bolts, leaving them with a hollow stick made from plants, and gave the lightning bolt to the people and taught them to set them on fire.

Zeus knew what Prometheus had done and decided to punish him, but Prometheus, known for his intellect, offered Zeus to share his flesh with people, on the condition that he let them hold fire, so Zeus agreed, and Prometheus presented Zeus with two proposals, one of which there was fresh meat, but placed in a disgusting gut, and others with sharp bones covered in meat, Zeus was deceived and chose the second proposal, so that the meat was left for people, and the bones for the great deity Zeus.

Zeus got angry with Prometheus and decided to punish him and bind him with iron chains in the Caucasus Mountains, and every morning the eagle of Zeus came and devoured the liver of Prometheus, and as an additional punishment he made Zeus the liver of Prometheus to grow whenever, the eagle devoured him, and the fact that Prometheus could predict the future predicted Pan. One of Zeus's sons would save him, and that he would come from the descendants of Zeus, who would kill him and put an end to his unjust rule.

Zeus asked Prometheus to tell him a prophecy about his death, but Prometheus refused to tell Zeus about it, and Zeus was angry with him and decided to send punishment to people, so he decided to give people another gift that could change the course of their whole life, and was " a woman ", so he asked Hephaestus to form a beautiful woman (From fire, he asked Athena to show endurance and asked Aphrodt to make her attractive in order to tear out her eyes, and asked Hermes to give her intelligence and superficial thinking, then Zeus called her" Pandora "(It was everything is given) Then Zeus sent Pandora to Avimetius and gave her a closed box, and he wrote "Do not open", Avimetheus was wise enough not to specifically accept a gift from Zeus, but Pandora's beauty forgot his wisdom, so he had to accept the gift and married Pandora after that.

Even after the wedding, Avimtius did not dare to open the box, but Pandora was curious, she took advantage of her husband's exit from the house and opened the box to get out of any bad quality that the world knew (hatred, hatred, poverty, murder) .. Etc. Pandora tried her best to close the box, but it was too late. Corruption redeemed on earth, people began to kill each other, wars broke out in all parts of the earth, and Zeus achieved his aspiration that he was looking for.

Generations passed generation after generation, and Hercules, son of Zeus, came and rescued Prometheus from his torment, so Zeus got angry because Prometheus escaped punishment for another, so he decided to send a flood to drown all of humanity. Prometheus predicted what Zeus would do, so he rushed to the people to warn them before it was too late.

Zeus sent a flood to people and did not survive for a couple who climbed to the top of Mount Bernassus (Decalion and his wife Viria), and after the period of the flood Viria gave birth to a child named "Helen", to whom the Greeks belonged.

In the end, Zeus agreed to pardon Prometheus on the condition that he made a ring of chains that bound him and wore it on his finger, and the latter did so, and from that day on, people wore rings in token of Prometheus's gratitude.

Finally

All of the above lines are Greek myths that are outdated and do not correspond to reality, although these myths are deprived of health, we cannot deny the ancient Greek civilization and its main role in the development of science and philosophy of all kinds.

AFRICA: LEGENDS OF FABULOUS OBJECTS!

Africa is a large continent the size of mountains, plains, beaches and rivers, which is also teeming with human beings, with human myths and multiple cysts, this mythology has emerged over the centuries and has been passed down from generation to generation between certified websites, this mythology is a stranger-this is what we will consider with you in the following lines, I hope it will not be boring, but God will start ..

People-eaters of trees!

Africa: Legends of Fairy Objects!

Trees in the world as a whole are useful and have many uses and benefits, for example, it is to purify the air and be from wood, which was previously a food source for many organisms, but what if I told you that there are trees that change to other objects , and not vice versa. trees eat people ?! ..

You may not believe this, and that trees change the process of photosynthesis, of course, your word is correct from a scientific point of view, but in Africa, namely on the island of Madagascar, people believe in people, things are far from science, they believe that trees are adults, and they heard the trees move, and also if you made the trees your own and you, like your tree, if you are a wooden boat made of the type of the tree itself, protects you from curses and evil spirits, there are also types of trees and use trees to catch people and them .. Lift them up, and then pick up their man's Wismar in the inner part of the trunk, this man's relatives and his friends will hear the farewell song of this unfortunate man, and the only way to save him is to pay the ransom to the university, and he, in his turn, will use its magical powers to open the tree and bring out a human victim.

Rose flower!

Africa: Legends of Fairy Objects!

Whether the words in Afrikaans (languages of South Africa) mean great snake, this snake lives in a cave called (hole of miracles) in the area of any field in South Africa.

Legend has it that there was a gigantic monster, very powerful, which made the gods, frightened by its power, divide it into two halves, the first half of the snake, and the second villa, but the object was identified with this plant, returned and returned again, and that the length of the object can reach six feet.

I assume that many people in the cave are a hole of wonders, which is full of diamonds due to the nature of South Africa and the frequent presence of diamonds in it, but no one is sure about this, because the area tends to protect the cave and not allow any more entrances.

- Not!

Africa: Legends of Fairy Objects!

The monstrous bird appeared in Congo, Angola and Zambia, the description of its appearance resembles a reptile, but a fly, classified for some kind of horror, was first written about it by an Englishman named Frank Welland in 1932.

Many Africans have seen him, they claimed that he lives on river banks and in swamps, maybe your funeral is huge, but without the blades, many theories say that Congress is a new species yet to be discovered, in some form The Dragon object is known in the folklore of most people, but some (the disabled) think it is just a Hollywood fairy tale.

Reality or myths? Other world games

The mirror and the devil's play

It is said that the best day for this game is Christmas, December 25 at 3 am, where the forces of darkness are known to be very active during this time.This game should light 12 candles next to the mirror and turn off all the lights. You look in the mirror without closing your eyes and say the word "demon" in Arabic or "Deval" in English or any other language, and within a short period of time, Satan's face will appear in the mirror! .. There is little information in this game because all those who tried this game became unnatural people, as if the game negatively influenced their minds or was acquired.

Korean Game: Elevator Into the Afterlife

All you have to do in this game is to follow some instructions, The first one is to search for a 10-story building with an elevator.Once you go to it, you call the elevator and then go up to the board and press the fourth floor button, and when it stops, do not go down from this, but press the second floor button and do not go down from it, but stay in your place, and then go back up to the elevator to the sixth floor, then go down to the second floor, and then go up to the tenth floor, then go down to fifth floor .. Then the elevator door will open and you will find a very beautiful girl, but do not look into her eyes and never look at her .. You will take the elevator and try to avoid it and press the button for the first floor, but this time you will notice that the elevator does not go down, but rises to the tenth floor, at the same time you have one chance to survive - to press any other button to avoid the button of the tenth layer .. Then everything disappears .. But if you cannot avoid it, you will find you are on the tenth floor and open the door to see a dark and frightening world, and you cannot return from it unless you do the same previous steps, but in the opposite way .. Some say that once you get out of the elevator, you cannot return to it and stay in another world.

Ouya game :

Ouija board - also known as message board or message board - this may be the most famous game that helps us communicate with the other world and has a lot of experience. It was made by an American businessman named Elijah Bond on July 1, 1890, and was considered a harmless parlor game until the American spiritualist Pearl Curran used it as a speculation tool during World War I.

It is a wooden board with letters written in English and numbers, and at the top of the board is the word "hello", at the bottom is the word "farewell", on the right side is the word "yes" and on the left side is the word "no". A small wooden pointer in the shape of a heart is used to convey the message of souls, where the participants in the game put their fingers on the cursor, then they ask a question to the ghost, The indicator moves according to the ghostly answer, By grouping letters, numbers and phrases on which the indicator stands, one can know that says the ghost. But be careful .. Before you think about playing this game, you should know that its consequences are sometimes severe, and there are many stories of people who were demonically abused .. And even death .. Because of the Ouija board .

Japanese game Daromsan :

Daromsan is a Japanese girl who fell into the bathroom of her house at night and hit her head on the ground, which led to her death .. It is said that if you turn off the light after midnight and go to the shower with cold water, then lie in the bathtub closed eyes and repeat the name Daromsan three times, you will feel that someone came up to you and put his hand on your body or found him standing behind you .. And this person is nothing but the ghost of the Daromsan girl! .. To escape from it, you have to do the pelvis very carefully and slowly so as not to harm you .. It is rumored that the ghost of the girl will accompany you during the day when you try and you will feel that someone is following you.

Midnight game :

This is a game in which you need a candle, salt and sulfur, and your book is your name on a white sheet, on which you put a drop of blood and leave it until the paper has completely absorbed it.Then you put the paper in front of the entrance to your house with a candle and knock on the door 12 ways and the last road is fully synchronized with the middle of the night, then you open the door and extinguish the candle and all that means that you have allowed the ghost of a midnight person to enter your house. After closing the door, the candle will be lit again and looks around your house at the ghost of a person.If the candle goes out automatically, it means that his soul has entered, Try to light the candle again within ten seconds, and if you cannot, draw a circle around you with salt, or you will be horrified and hallucinated .. They say that the game ends at 15:33 .. Where the souls of another world disappear, it is also not allowed to put your blood on the name of another person, because this provokes a ghost, and you do not know what might happen.

www.ingramcontent.com/pod-product-compliance
Lightning Source LLC
Chambersburg PA
CBHW061538120726
48001CB00004B/1620